The Kalahari Typing School for Men

ALEXANDER McCALL SMITH

Level 4

Retold by Annette Keen
Series Editors: Andy Hopkins and Jocelyn Potter

Pearson Education Limited
Edinburgh Gate, Harlow,
Essex CM20 2JE, England
and Associated Companies throughout the world.

ISBN: 978-1-4058-9213-1

This edition first published by Pearson Education Ltd 2009

3 5 7 9 10 8 6 4

Text copyright © Pearson Education Ltd 2009
Illustrations by Doreen Lang

Set in 11/14pt Bembo
Printed in China
SWTC/03

The moral rights of the authors have been asserted in accordance with
the Copyright Designs and Patents Act 1988

Published by Pearson Education Limited in association with
Penguin Books Ltd, and both companies being subsidiaries of Pearson PLC

For a complete list of the titles available in the Penguin Readers series please write to your local
Pearson Longman office or to: Penguin Readers Marketing Department, Pearson Education,
Edinburgh Gate, Harlow, Essex CM20 2JE, England.

Contents

Introduction

Precious Ramotswe had become used to being the only private detective in town, in fact the only one in the whole country. She had not expected competition. But she was not a woman to give up easily.

... 'There's one other thing,' said Mma Makutsi. 'These detectives are men.'

'Ah,' said Mma Ramotswe. 'That is a good thing, and a bad thing too.'

Life at the No.*1 Ladies' Detective Agency becomes more difficult with the surprising arrival of a new detective in town. *Ex-CID†. Ex-New York. Ex-cellent!* reads the sign outside the new agency, and the owner certainly sounds experienced. But will he be able to solve the kinds of cases that come to Mma‡ Ramotswe? Daily life in Botswana is not like New York, and the people are not the same either. Mma Ramotswe has the advantage because she understands the local people, their traditions and their problems. But competition must always be taken seriously ...

And Mma Ramotswe is not the only one with problems to solve: her secretary, Mma Makutsi, has difficulties in *her* life too. First, there is the question of how to earn more money, and then there is the problem of finding a husband. Time is running out if she wants to meet a man of her own age. So where should she look, and what sort of man is she looking for?

---

* no.: short for *number*

† CID: a group of police detectives that were feared in South Africa under white governments

‡ Mma: *Mrs* or *Madam* in Setswana, the language spoken by most people in Botswana

In *The Kalahari Typing School for Men*, Mma Ramotswe needs all her intelligence and understanding to bring satisfactory solutions to her clients, and Mma Makutsi finds that the simplest ideas are often the best. With the help of many cups of red bush tea*, life at the No.1 Ladies' Detective Agency continues in its gentle, unhurried way, guided by the wise and sensible Precious Ramotswe.

Alexander McCall Smith was born in Zimbabwe, and grew up there until he left to study at university in Scotland. He returned to Africa to teach law at the University of Botswana, and his love of the country comes through clearly in his books. His characters are not just invented; he has known many people like Mma Ramotswe, Mr JLB Matekoni and their friends.

He returned to Scotland to teach medical law at Edinburgh University. During his working life he has written more than fifty non-fiction books, but *The No.1 Ladies' Detective Agency* was his first mystery story. It appeared in 1999 and was an immediate success. Other books followed. McCall Smith has said that he could not leave Mma Ramotswe at the end of the first book. 'It seemed rather rude,' he says. 'Like getting up in the middle of a conversation and leaving the room.'

The books have been translated into thirty-nine languages and have sold over fourteen million copies around the world – including in Botswana, where they are very popular. In 2004, the *No.1 Ladies' Detective Agency* books won two prizes for British writers. There have now been nine books about Mma Ramotswe's detective agency. McCall Smith's millions of readers wait for each new book to appear, happy to read as much as he wants to write about Mma Ramotswe and her friends. 'People enjoy the books,' McCall Smith has said, 'and it's almost

* red bush tea: a South African tea made from red leaves

unkind to say that I'm not going to write any more.'

Alexander McCall Smith now lives in Edinburgh with his wife Elizabeth, a doctor. He has also written other fiction, including the *44 Scotland Street* and the *Portuguese Irregular Verbs* books.

Many people have learnt about the beautiful country of Botswana through McCall Smith's stories. It is a small country in southern Africa with fewer than two million people. Most of Botswana is covered by the Kalahari Desert, and it is home to many different animals and birds, which tourists come to see. Britain governed Botswana from 1885 until 1966, when Botswana became independent. Now, the economy is growing and the capital, Gaborone, is the fastest-growing city in Africa.

But like all African countries, Botswana has its problems. Many people suffer from AIDS*. There is more crime than before. As the country becomes more modern, the traditional way of life is disappearing, and the attitudes of younger people are not the same as the attitudes of their parents and grandparents. Change is happening quickly.

Mma Ramotswe and her friends are proud of modern Botswana, but they try to live by the traditional values. Away from Gabarone the real Botswana can still be found, and Mma Ramotswe loves her journeys out into the country in her little white van.

Africa is an important part of these books, and it is impossible to imagine the stories placed in any other part of the world. Thanks to Mma Ramotswe, many people have learnt about Botswana, and understand what makes it such a wonderful country.

There are other Penguin Readers about Mma Ramotswe and her friends. Look for *The No.1 Ladies' Detective Agency* (Level 3) and *Tears of the Giraffe* (Level 4).

* AIDS: a very serious disease that often causes death

ZAMBIA

ANGOLA

ZIMBABWE

NAMIBIA

Okavango

BOTSWANA

KALAHARI
DESERT

Mochudi

Molepolole

GABORONE

Lobatse

SOUTH AFRICA

0   100 km

AFRICA

BOTSWANA

Chapter 1
How to Find a Man and a Business Idea

'I must remember,' thought Mma Ramotswe, 'how lucky I am in this life.' Sitting in the garden of her house in Zebra Drive, and looking up at the high, blue Botswana sky, Precious Ramotswe thought about the things that made her life so fortunate.

She was the owner of Botswana's only detective agency, the No. 1 Ladies' Detective Agency, which successfully kept almost all of its clients happy. (There were some clients, she knew, who could never be satisfied.) Still only in her late thirties, Mma Ramotswe had her house in Botswana's capital, Gaborone. She had two orphan children, a boy and a girl, to bring life and fun into the house. With these things in her life, she could honestly say that nothing more was needed.

But there was more. Some time ago Mma Ramotswe had agreed to marry Mr JLB Matekoni, the owner of Tlokweng Road Speedy Motors. He was thought to be the best mechanic in Botswana, a good man and a gentle one.

Mr JLB Matekoni could not be described as an exciting man, but he was not dull either. Mma Ramotswe had been married once before, to a man who many girls would think of as exciting, and she did not want excitement again. No, she thought, Mr JLB Matekoni was perfect; you could sit with him for hours and although he might not say anything very important, he was certainly not boring. Of course he talked a lot about cars. He thought they had their own personalities, and he could tell just by looking at a car what sort of owner it had.

Mma Ramotswe and Mr JLB Matekoni had met thanks to her little white van. He had repaired it for her, and afterwards she had often visited him at the garage. Then one morning the little white van had refused to start, and Mr JLB Matekoni had spent a whole afternoon at Zebra Drive with the engine in a hundred pieces. After he had put everything back together and they were drinking tea in the house, Mr JLB Matekoni had asked Mma Ramotswe to marry him, and she had agreed.

It was a great surprise to Mma Ramotswe when Mr JLB Matekoni became ill. His illness was not one of the body; instead, it was his mind that was affected. He had become sad and had lost interest in the Tlokweng Road garage. It seemed to Mma Ramotswe that the real Mr JLB Matekoni had simply left his body and gone somewhere else.

During his illness Mma Ramotswe's assistant, Mma Makutsi, had kept the garage running. She had made great improvements to it. She made the lazy apprentices work harder, and a large number of women started coming to the garage. More and more women had their own cars now, and they were pleased to take them to a garage run by a woman.

Thanks to Dr Moffat, and the drug treatment he suggested, Mr JLB Matekoni's health had slowly improved. He started to smile again and his familiar personality returned. He began to take an interest in the garage business and talked of returning to it.

'What are we going to do to thank Mma Makutsi?' asked Mma Ramotswe. 'She's put so much work into the garage, and when you are back she is just going to be an assistant manager and an assistant private detective again. It will be hard for her.'

'I would not like to upset her,' said Mr JLB Matekoni. 'You are right about her work. She has paid all the bills on time, and organised everything in the office. Even the garage floor is cleaner.'

'Her life is not very good,' said Mma Ramotswe. 'She is living in that one room with a sick brother. I cannot pay her very much. And she has no husband to look after her. She deserves better than that.'

Mr JLB Matekoni could help financially by allowing her to continue as Assistant Manager at Tlokweng Road Speedy Motors, but he could not help with the question of a husband. This was women's business, he thought. Surely Mma Ramotswe could tell her how to find a husband?

Mma Ramotswe was not at all sure about this. 'You have to be careful what you say,' she said. 'You can't just go and tell someone like Mma Makutsi that they know nothing about how to find a husband. She got ninety-seven per cent in her final examination at secretarial college – she's an intelligent woman.'

'It doesn't matter about her ninety-seven per cent,' said Mr JLB Matekoni. 'You could get one hundred per cent for typing and still not know how to talk to men. Marriage is different from typing. Quite different.'

Mma Ramotswe was wondering when she and Mr JLB Matekoni might get married themselves. But Dr Moffat had warned against making too many decisions too soon, so she said nothing about wedding dates. It was clear that Mr JLB Matekoni was worried about Mma Makutsi, so eventually Mma Ramotswe agreed to speak to her some time soon about finding a husband.

♦

During Mr JLB Matekoni's illness they had moved the No.1 Ladies' Detective Agency into the back office at Tlokweng Road Speedy Motors. It was a successful arrangement. There was a separate entrance for Agency clients, and the garage could easily be organised from there. Sometimes, clients arriving for one business found that they needed the services of the other one too.

Now, with the day's post of four letters attended to, Mma Ramotswe suggested to her assistant that it was time for a cup of bush tea. Mma Makutsi made the tea and put a cup on her employer's desk.

'Mma Makutsi,' Mma Ramotswe began, 'are you happy?'

Mma Makutsi was surprised, and worried. She lived in fear of losing her job and it seemed to her that this question might be leading in that direction. Life was unfair, she thought. The best jobs went to the beautiful girls, even the ones who only got fifty per cent in their examinations at secretarial college.

'I am very happy,' Mma Makutsi said, sadly. 'I am happy with this job. I don't want to go anywhere else.'

Mma Ramotswe laughed. 'Oh, the job. We know you're happy with the job, and we are very happy with you. Everyone knows you are our right-hand woman.'

Mma Makutsi felt more relaxed now as she drank her tea.

'But are you happy in yourself?' continued Mma Ramotswe. 'Are you getting what you want out of life?'

'I'm not sure what I want out of life. I used to think I would like to be rich, but I've met some rich people now and I'm not so sure about that.'

'Happiness and money are not connected,' said Mma Ramotswe.

Mma Makutsi agreed. 'Now I think that happiness comes from somewhere inside,' she said. 'Happiness is in the head.'

'And in the heart?' Mma Ramotswe suggested.

There was a silence. Mma Makutsi looked down at her desk. 'The heart is the place where love happens,' she said quietly.

Mma Ramotswe took a deep breath. 'Would you like to have a husband? Someone to look after you and make you happier?' she asked, gently.

Mma Makutsi took off her glasses and cleaned them with her handkerchief.

'I would like to have a husband,' she said. 'But there are many beautiful girls. They are the ones getting the husbands. There is nobody left for me.'

'Perhaps you should be doing a bit more about it if no men

4

are coming your way,' said Mma Ramotswe. 'Try to find one.'

'Where?' asked Mma Makutsi. 'Where are all these men?'

Mma Ramotswe waved a hand in the direction of the door, and of Africa outside. 'Out there. You have to meet them.'

'Where exactly?' asked Mma Makutsi.

'In the middle of the town. You see them every day sitting about at lunchtime. Men. Plenty of them.'

'All married,' said Mma Makutsi.

'Or in bars,' said Mma Ramotswe, feeling that the conversation was not going the way she had planned.

'Bars are full of men looking for bad girls,' said Mma Makutsi, and Mma Ramotswe had to agree.

'It is kind of you to think of me like this,' said Mma Makutsi. 'But you and Mr JLB Matekoni must not worry about me. I am happy enough, and if there is someone out there for me, I am sure we will meet one day.'

Mma Ramotswe let the conversation end there. But she thought that Mma Makutsi should make more of herself. She was a citizen of Botswana, which was a very fine thing to be, because Botswana had never done anything to feel ashamed of. She had passed her examination at the Botswana Secretarial College with ninety-seven per cent. She lived in the capital city, Gaborone, far from the little village where she was born, so she had progressed.

Mma Ramotswe looked up at Mma Makutsi, who was now busy typing a letter. 'Mr JLB Matekoni and I must try to help her,' she thought. 'She is a fine woman with many great skills. She deserves a better life, and we must help her to find one.'

♦

Things were returning to normal at Tlokweng Road Speedy Motors. Mr JLB Matekoni was at the garage by seven each morning and his two apprentices were there by eight o'clock.

He could see that they had improved under the careful eye of Mma Makutsi.

'Those two boys are working much better,' he said to Mma Ramotswe. 'The older boy still talks all the time about girls, but their work is cleaner and more careful. I think they learnt something while I was away.'

There were other changes too. Charlie, the older apprentice, said that the younger boy had become very religious. He had stopped thinking all the time about girls, and was now an enthusiastic member of a local church.

The apprentices were a mystery to Mr JLB Matekoni. He didn't understand them and would be glad when their studying ended and they left him to get a job at another garage. Life was much more complicated now for Mr JLB Matekoni. In the past it had been simple: he had been alone at the garage, and had only himself to think about. Now there were two apprentices, Mma Makutsi and Mma Ramotswe – and that was without the two orphan children at Zebra Drive. He had arranged for Mma Ramotswe to take them as foster children, so in a way he was responsible for them too. It was a big step, from one person to six.

While Mr JLB Matekoni imagined that he was responsible for others, they imagined that they were responsible for him. Mma Makutsi had thought a lot since her conversation with Mma Ramotswe, when she had feared her job was in danger. The No.1 Ladies' Detective Agency didn't make much money. The garage did better, but the apprentices had to be paid, and that took a lot of money each month. The banks were charging more and more, so the businesses had to make more money. In her opinion, they needed a new business idea. One morning, she suddenly thought of something. Mma Ramotswe and Mr JLB Matekoni were both out of the office, so she took her cup of bush tea into the garage and spoke to the two boys.

'I have a plan,' she said, 'and I wondered what you thought of it. It's a simple idea.'

'I have simple ideas too,' said Charlie, the older apprentice. 'I have ideas of girls. Simple. Girls, and then more girls.'

Mma Makutsi pretended that she hadn't heard him.

'There are many people wanting to learn how to drive, are there not?' she asked.

The younger apprentice spoke. 'They can learn on the bush roads. There are lots of places for them to practise.'

'But that won't help them drive in town,' said Mma Makutsi quickly. 'There are too many things happening in town. There are cars going this way and that. There are people crossing the road.'

'And lots of girls,' said Charlie. 'Lots of girls walking about. All the time.'

'So,' Mma Makutsi continued, 'I have decided that we should open a driving school. I do not think there are enough of them. We can start a new one, and give people lessons after work. We could charge forty pula★ a lesson. Twenty pula to Mr JLB Matekoni for the garage and for using his car, and twenty pula to the teacher. It would be a great success.'

The older apprentice was not interested. 'I want to see my friends after work,' he said. 'I do not have time to take people for driving lessons.'

Mma Makutsi looked at his friend. 'And you?'

The younger apprentice smiled at her. 'You are a very clever lady, Mma. I think this is a good idea.'

'There!' said Mma Makutsi to Charlie. 'You see your friend has a more positive way of looking at things. You are no use at all. Look what has happened to your brain with all those thoughts of girls.'

★ pula: the money of Botswana

7

'I will have to think of a good name for the school,' Mma Makutsi continued. 'The name is very important in business. That is why the No.1 Ladies' Detective Agency has been a success. The name says everything you need to know about the business.'

The younger apprentice looked at her. 'I have a good idea for the name,' he said. 'We could call it Learn to Drive with Jesus.'

There was a silence. The older apprentice looked at his friend, then looked away.

'I am not sure about that,' said Mma Makutsi. 'I will think about it, but I am not sure.'

'It is a very good name,' said the younger apprentice. 'It will bring us more careful drivers and that will mean we have no accidents.'

'I will talk to Mr JLB Matekoni about it and see what he thinks,' said Mma Makutsi. 'Thank you for the suggestion.'

Chapter 2 Problems with the Children

Mma Ramotswe completed her shopping. Before the two orphans came to stay, shopping had been easy and she had rarely had to shop more than once a week. Now it seemed she was shopping much more often. The girl, Motholeli, liked to bake cakes, and her brother, Puso, certainly liked to eat them. As soon as Mma Ramotswe bought more eggs and sugar, they were used, and the resulting cakes were eaten almost immediately. All this extra food cost a lot of money, and it was only thanks to Mr JLB Matekoni that she was able to afford it.

It had been Mr JLB Matekoni's idea to foster the children. He had not been able to say no when Mma Silvia Potokwani, Matron of the orphan farm, had asked him. She had probably realised that the children would actually live in Mma Ramotswe's house in Zebra Drive, instead of Mr JLB Matekoni's house near the old Botswana Defence Club. Of course, after the marriage (whenever that would be) they would all live together under the same roof. The children had already asked about that, and Mma Ramotswe had said she was waiting for Mr JLB Matekoni to decide on a date.

'He does not rush things,' she had explained. 'Mr JLB Matekoni is a very careful man. He likes to do things slowly.'

She realised that Puso needed a father and didn't want to wait too much longer to get one. At the age of six a week was a long time; a month would be impossible for him to imagine.

Motholeli was older and she understood. She was disabled, and had to use a wheelchair all the time because she could not walk. She was used to waiting, and it took her a long time to do most things, much longer than other children. She was usually a cheerful girl, though, so when Mma Ramotswe returned from her shopping trip and heard no happy greeting from Motholeli, she was surprised.

Mma Ramotswe put her shopping bags onto the table. 'So much shopping,' she said. 'Meat, rice and vegetables.' She paused. She knew that Motholeli liked chicken. 'And a chicken,' she added. 'A nice fat one.'

At first the girl said nothing. Then she replied, in a quiet voice: 'That is good.'

Mma Ramotswe looked at her. That morning Motholeli had left the house in a cheerful mood, so it seemed something had happened at school. Mma Ramotswe remembered events from her own school days – big things at the time, but they seemed so small and unimportant now. People said that school days were happy, but they were often not. For some children it was like being in a prison; frightened of older children and teachers, and unable to talk to anybody about it because they thought nobody would understand. Some things were better now, of course. Teachers were not allowed to hit children, although Mma Ramotswe thought that for some boys a little

'I do not have to be a detective to know that.'

physical correction might be a good thing. Mr JLB Matekoni's apprentices, for example, might improve with such treatment. She thought about the idea of coming up behind the older apprentice when he was bending over to change a tyre, and kicking his bottom. How enjoyable it would be to do that and then to say: 'Let that be a lesson!'

But these were not serious thoughts and did not help the immediate problem. Mma Ramotswe put away the last of her shopping and then made some red bush tea. She sat down.

'You're unhappy,' she said to Motholeli. 'And it's something at school, isn't it?'

Motholeli shook her head. 'No,' she said. 'I am not unhappy.'

'That is not true,' said Mma Ramotswe. 'You are a happy girl usually. You are famous for your happiness. And now you are almost crying. I do not have to be a detective to know that.'

The girl looked down at the ground. 'I have no mother,' she said quietly. 'I am a girl who has no mother.'

So that was it. Mma Ramotswe understood this feeling. Motholeli was missing her mother in exactly the same way she, Precious Ramotswe, missed her own mother and father, now both dead. She crossed the kitchen floor and put her arms around Motholeli.

'Of course you have a mother, Motholeli. She is watching you from heaven all the time, and she is thinking, "I am very proud of that fine girl, my daughter. I am proud of how hard she is working and how she is looking after her little brother."'

She felt Motholeli's warm tears against her own skin. 'You mustn't cry, and you mustn't be unhappy,' she said. 'Your mother would not want you to be unhappy, would she?'

'She doesn't care. She doesn't care what happens to me.'

Mma Ramotswe looked at the child. 'That is not true. Of course she cares.'

11

'No. There is a girl at school telling me that I have no mother because my mother did not like me and so she left.'

'And who is this girl?' asked Mma Ramotswe angrily. 'Who is telling you all these lies?'

'She is a very popular girl at school. She is a rich girl. She has many friends and they all believe the things she says.'

'Her name?' said Mma Ramotswe. 'What is the name of this popular girl?' Motholeli gave the name. 'We will talk more about this later,' said Mma Ramotswe. 'But you must remember that these things are not true. It doesn't matter who this girl is. You lost your mother because she was sick. She was a good woman. I asked Mma Potokwani about her and that is what she told me. She said your mother was a strong woman who was kind to people. You remember that and be proud of it.'

Motholeli lifted her head and looked at Mma Ramotswe.

'And there is something else you must remember,' said Mma Ramotswe. 'Every person in Botswana is of equal value. The same. That means you too. You may be an orphan girl, but you are as good as anyone else. Nobody can look at you and say, "I am better than you." Remember that for the rest of your life.'

Motholeli had stopped crying, and Mma Ramotswe stood up.

'Now,' she said, 'we should start cooking this fine chicken so that when Mr JLB Matekoni comes to have dinner with us this evening we shall have a good meal ready for him on the table. Would you like that?'

Motholeli smiled. 'I would like that very much, Mma,' she said.

♦

Mr JLB Matekoni left the garage at five o'clock and drove straight to the house in Zebra Drive. He liked the early evening, when the heat had gone out of the sun. It was pleasant to walk about in the last hour or two before it started to get dark. Tonight he planned to spend some time in Mma Ramotswe's vegetable garden at the back of the house. He had already planted some beans there, and in a dry country like Botswana it was difficult to make sure they had enough water. The ground was always so thirsty, and plants needed watering regularly.

Mr JLB Matekoni filled a bucket from the tap at the back of the house. Inside the kitchen, Mma Ramotswe heard the tap running and looked out of the window. She waved to him, and he waved back before he carried the water to the bean plants.

Mma Ramotswe smiled to herself and thought, 'Here I am at last, with a good man, who is happy to work in the garden and grow beans for me.' It was a thought that made her feel warm with pleasure.

Mr JLB Matekoni poured a little water carefully around each plant. He bent down to examine one of the smaller plants, and there was a sudden noise behind him. It sounded like a stone hitting something, followed by a small movement. He turned immediately – a noise like that could easily be a snake, and some snakes could kill a man with one bite.

It was not a snake, but a small, beautifully coloured bird. It was still moving a little but soon stopped. He picked up the small body and saw at once the place where it had been hit by a stone.

Boys, he thought. It would be boys with their catapults, killing birds not to eat but just for sport. He shouted across the fence and into the bush at the end of the garden, 'I saw you kill this bird!' – but he knew they would already be gone.

When Mr JLB Matekoni went back to the house, he found Mma Ramotswe waiting for him at the kitchen door.

'Have you seen Puso?' she asked. 'He was playing in the garden but now it is dinner time and he has not come back.'

'I have not seen him. I have been in the garden ...' He stopped. 'And? Is he there?'

13

Mr JLB Matekoni paused for a moment.

'I think he is. I think he is using a catapult out there.'

They both went to the end of the garden and looked over the fence into the bush.

'Puso!' called Mma Ramotswe. 'We know that you are hiding. Come out or I shall come and get you myself.'

They waited for a few moments. Then Mma Ramotswe called out again. 'Puso! We know you are there!'

'I am not here.' The boy's voice was very clear. 'I am not.'

'How can you say you are not there?' said Mma Ramotswe. 'Who is speaking if it is not you?'

There was a further silence, then the small boy came out from under a large bush.

'He killed a bird with his catapult,' whispered Mr JLB Matekoni. 'I saw it.'

The boy walked towards them, his head down.

'Go to your room, Puso,' said Mma Ramotswe, 'and stay there until we call you.'

The boy looked up. His face was wet with tears.

'I hate you,' he said. Then he turned to Mr JLB Matekoni. 'And I hate you too.'

He ran towards the house, past the two shocked adults, not looking back at them as he ran.

Chapter 3   A New Detective in Town

Nothing seemed to be going well for Mma Ramotswe. First, there was that difficult evening with the children. Motholeli's problems still had to be solved, but at least she was more cheerful after their talk. Puso was quite different, though. He had just shut them out, refusing to eat. It seemed they could say nothing that made any difference. They had not punished him after the

14

problem with the dead bird, but he was not at all grateful for that. Was this how orphan children behaved? Mma Ramotswe knew that these children had often been damaged in their early lives and were sometimes difficult, but they had only ever given Puso love and support and he had seemed quite happy before. She decided to go and see Mma Potokwani at the orphan farm and ask her advice.

There was more bad news waiting for her the following day when she arrived at the office. She had been hoping for a quiet day with no problems, but Mma Makutsi had something important to tell her.

'I have been sitting here for the last hour, wanting to cry,' she said.

'You had better tell me,' said Mma Ramotswe. 'What has happened?'

'I went shopping yesterday,' Mma Makutsi began, 'and in one of the empty shops I saw someone putting up a new sign. I looked through the window, and saw a lot of new office furniture.'

She stopped and looked around her at the old furniture in the No.1 Ladies' Detective Agency office. Mma Ramotswe thought there was going to be a request for new furniture. It would be impossible, she thought. The business was losing money and it was only because of the connection with Tlokweng Road Speedy Motors that they kept going. She lifted a hand.

'I'm sorry, Mma Makutsi,' she said. 'We simply don't have the money for new equipment here.'

Mma Makutsi stared at her. 'That is not what I was going to say,' she said. 'I was going to say something quite different. Something much more important.'

'I'm sorry,' said Mma Ramotswe. 'Tell me what you saw.'

'A new detective agency,' said Mma Makutsi. 'It is called the Satisfaction Guaranteed Detective Agency.'

This was certainly surprising news. Mma Ramotswe had

become used to being the only private detective in town, in fact the only one in the whole country. She had not expected competition. But she was not a woman to give up easily.

'Every business must expect competition,' she said. 'We are no different.'

'That is true,' replied Mma Makutsi. 'At the Botswana Secretarial College they taught us that competition is healthy. And they said that you must know what the competition is. We should go and take a look at these new people and see what they are doing.'

Mma Ramotswe picked up the keys to her little white van.

'You are right, Mma Makutsi. We'll go and introduce ourselves.'

'There's one other thing,' said Mma Makutsi. 'These detectives are men.'

'Ah,' said Mma Ramotswe. 'That is a good thing, and a bad thing too.'

♦

It was not difficult to find the Satisfaction Guaranteed Detective Agency. There was a very large sign, with the name at the top and a picture of a smiling man behind a desk. Underneath this picture was painted in large, red letters: *Ex-CID. Ex-New York. Ex-cellent!*

Mma Ramotswe parked the little white van on the opposite side of the street and they looked across at the agency.

'Ex-CID,' said Mma Ramotswe. 'He used to be a policeman. People will love the idea of taking their problems to him.'

'And ex-New York,' said Mma Makutsi. 'People have seen films about New York detectives and they know how good they are.'

'We'll go in and introduce ourselves,' said Mma Ramotswe.

They crossed the road and went up to the door. There was a sign on it that said: *Please enter. No need to knock.* But Mma

Ramotswe believed in the traditional values – it was the correct thing to knock on a door before entering, and so she knocked.

'No need to knock, Mma,' said a man sitting behind a desk. 'Just come in.'

'I always knock, Rra★. It is the right thing to do.'

The man smiled. 'In my business,' he said, 'it's not always a good idea to knock. People stop what they're doing. But as you can see, I am doing nothing bad. Just sitting here waiting for two beautiful ladies like you to come in and see me.'

'I am not called beautiful every day, Rra. It is nice when that happens,' said Mma Ramotswe.

He looked at Mma Ramotswe again, and then suddenly seemed to recognise her.

'You are Mma Ramotswe, aren't you? The No.1 Ladies' Detective Agency? I have seen your picture in the newspaper. And you are Mma …'

'Makutsi,' said Mma Makutsi. 'I am an assistant detective at the No.1 Ladies' Detective Agency. I was at the Botswana Secretarial College before …'

The man interrupted her. 'Oh, that place. Yes.'

Mma Ramotswe noticed the effect this had on Mma Makutsi. She breathed in sharply and narrowed her eyes at the insult.

'A fine college,' said Mma Ramotswe, quickly. 'But what is your name, Rra?'

'I am Cephas Buthelezi. Ex-CID, Johannesburg.'

They shook hands, and sat down. Mr Buthelezi took a cigarette from a packet on his desk. He did not offer one to his guests – neither of them smoked, but it was impolite and both ladies noticed it.

'And I see from your sign that you have lived in New York too,' said Mma Ramotswe.

★ Rra: *Sir* or *Mr* in Setswana

17

Mr Buthelezi looked away, remembering perhaps a more interesting life. 'Yes, New York. I have been in New York.'

'Did you like living in New York?' asked Mma Makutsi. 'I have always wanted to go there.'

'New York is a very big city,' said Mr Buthelezi. 'My God! Wow! There are many buildings there.'

'How many years did you live there?'

'Not many years.'

'How many?' asked Mma Makutsi.

'You are very interested in New York, Mma. You should go there and see it with your own eyes,' said Mr Buthelezi.

For a few moments there was silence, and Mma Makutsi's unanswered question – how long? – was left hanging in the air.

Mr Buthelezi blew his cigarette smoke up towards the ceiling. He seemed comfortable with the silence, but after a few moments he reached forward and passed a piece of paper to Mma Ramotswe.

'This is my brochure, Mma,' he said. 'I am happy for you to see it. I do not mind that there is more than one detective agency in this town. It's growing so quickly, isn't it? There is work for two of us.'

Mma Makutsi felt angry. 'And what about me?' she thought 'Are there not three of us, or am I just a nothing in your eyes?'

Mma Ramotswe took the brochure. There were pictures and some writing. 'Trust your enquiries to a MAN!' it said. Silently, she passed the brochure to Mma Makutsi.

'It has been very good to meet you, Rra,' said Mma Ramotswe, getting to her feet. 'We must meet again to discuss our cases.'

Mr Buthelezi smiled widely. 'That would be very good, Mma. You and me talking about professional matters ...'

'And Mma Makutsi,' said Mma Ramotswe.

'Ah, yes, of course,' said Mr Buthelezi, as they walked to the door.

When the two women were outside, they crossed the road in complete silence. Nothing at all was said until they were in the little white van and driving home.

'So,' said Mma Ramotswe.

Mma Makutsi searched for something to say, but could find nothing that showed how angry she was. So she too said, 'So.'

They returned to the office in silence. Mma Makutsi could see that Mma Ramotswe was as angry as she was. Mr Buthelezi had suggested that he had all the experience and she was new to the detective business. And there was the brochure, which Mma Makutsi still had in her hand. If some people wanted to speak to a man that was their decision, but it was quite another thing to suggest that men were always better detectives than women.

When they were back in the office, Mma Makutsi attended to the garage bills, and Mma Ramotswe tried to write a letter. But she could not keep her mind on it, and after twenty minutes of trying she went outside.

A small group of cows were eating grass at the side of the road, and a young boy was trying to make them move on. He called out to the cows by name: 'Broken Ear! Thin one! Come on, move!'

Mma Ramotswe watched the boy and the cows for a time, until a car turned off the road and parked next to her little white van. The driver, a tall man in his early forties, got out and asked her for the No.1 Ladies' Detective Agency. Mma Ramotswe realised she probably looked dreamy and not at all like a professional detective.

'That is me, Rra. I am sorry, I was watching the boy with the cows. I was not paying attention.'

The man laughed. 'And what is wrong with watching cows? I can look at cows for hours. You could be an animal detective, asking the cows to tell you things.'

Mma Ramotswe laughed. She liked this man immediately – he was the complete opposite of Mr Buthelezi.

'I must tell you my name,' said the man. 'I am Molefelo, and I come from Lobatse. I am an engineer, but I have a hotel down there too. I used to build things, but now I just sit in an office and organise other people. It is not as much fun, I'm afraid.'

'We can go into the office,' said Mma Ramotswe, pointing to the door. 'My assistant will make us tea and we can talk.'

Mr Molefelo looked at the office, where he could see Mma Makutsi looking out at him.

'I wonder if we could stay outside,' he began. 'Actually, I am going to say some very private things. Very, very private. Could we take a walk perhaps? I could talk while we are walking.'

As they walked along a path at the back of the garage, Mr Molefelo talked and Mma Ramotswe listened.

'I am a man who has changed,' said Mr Molefelo. 'Something happened to me two months ago and it has made me think about my whole life. I have thought about the things I did in the past, and how I should live my life in the future. I'm just an ordinary man,' he continued. 'I have done some bad things and some good things, but there is something I want to try to put right now.'

Mma Ramotswe waited for him to tell his story. Nothing shocked her now, although she was sometimes surprised at the way people complicated their lives.

'I have not told anybody else about the bad thing I did,' said Mr Molefelo, 'and before I tell you, I want you to understand why I need to do so now. As I said, I have a hotel in Lobatse. It has been very successful, and I used some of the money I made to buy a farm down near the border with Namibia. There I have many ostriches. I don't go to the farm often as it is a very long journey, but I went there recently with my wife and two sons.

'On the second night we were there some men came to the farm in the middle of the night. They were thieves, very dangerous men, and they wanted to steal my ostriches. Men like these come over the border from Namibia. They have guns and they are not afraid to use them. I woke in the night and heard noises. I thought it was perhaps a wild animal coming to eat the ostriches, so I took my gun and I went out to the fields.

'I had almost reached the ostrich field when I was hit over the head and knocked to the ground. I looked up and saw a man pointing a gun at my head, and I thought I was going to die. I thought of my sons and what would happen to them without a father. I thought of my own father. Some of the other thieves came to see what was happening and there was a discussion in a language I could not understand. I think they were trying to decide whether to kill me. Then I saw a light, and heard one of my men shout out from the house. One of the thieves hit me on the head with his gun, then they all ran to their horses and were gone. I was left with blood running down my face, and you can still see the marks here.'

Mr Molefelo pointed to the side of his face.

'You were a very lucky man,' said Mma Ramotswe.

'Yes, I was. But I was very shocked by those events, and when I faced death it made me look back at my life. I decided then that I wanted to put right the bad thing I did many years ago. And that is why I need your help, Mma.'

Chapter 4 Old Typewriters, New Beginnings

Mma Makutsi watched Mma Ramotswe walk away with Mr Molefelo and thought, 'This is the problem with being only an assistant detective. I don't speak to the clients personally; I hear about conversations second-hand. I am really just a secretary, not an assistant detective.' She turned to the garage bills on her desk and thought, 'I am not really an assistant garage manager either; I am a garage secretary, which is a different

21

thing completely.'

Mma Makutsi made herself some bush tea. Even if a client had arrived, there was no guarantee that his problem would become an actual, full-paid investigation. She knew that the future of the agency, and her job, was doubtful. Mma Ramotswe and Mr JLB Matekoni paid her as generously as they could, but it was only just enough for her to live on. She had to send money home to her parents, and then there was her rent and the money needed to buy medicines for her brother.

She realised that the only way of improving her situation was to take on extra work in her free time. The driving school had been a good idea, but when she thought more about it she could see that the costs would be high. She needed another plan.

Mma Makutsi started to type a letter. Suddenly, as she typed, the idea came to her, and she knew immediately that it was a good one. Most typists, she thought, were women. At the Botswana Secretarial College there were only women learning to type. But men needed to type too if they wanted to use computers. And why did they not learn to type correctly, instead of with just one finger? It was, she realised, because they didn't want to be in a class with a lot of girls who would probably be better than them. So why not have a typing school just for men? Mma Makutsi could easily teach them herself. She typed the words to see how they looked: Grace P. Makutsi, Principal, Kalahari Typing School for Men.

They looked very good, and Mma Makutsi was certain the idea would work. Of course, there were some problems to solve first.

For a start, there was the question of money. Mma Makutsi had only enough money to buy one second-hand typewriter, and she would need at least ten. She could not afford to borrow the money from a bank. There seemed to be no way of solving this problem. It was a fact that to make money, one needed to

So why not have a typing school just for men?

have money in the first place.

Then a thought came to her. Typewriters! Who had a large number of old typewriters collecting dust in a cupboard? The Botswana Secretarial College!

Mma Makutsi picked up the phone and called her friend Mma Manapotsi, the Assistant Principal at the College. They exchanged warm greetings first, then Mma Makutsi explained her idea and asked about the unused typewriters.

'Of course,' said Mma Manapotsi. 'Why not? Those old machines are useless and we need to clear the space. There are about twelve,' she continued. 'They don't work very well, you know. They go *qwertyui* instead of *qwertyuiop*★. Some of them even go *qop*.'

'I don't mind,' said Mma Makutsi. 'They're only for men.'

'Well, that's all right then,' said Mma Manapotsi.

After she had put the phone down, Mma Makutsi celebrated by dancing round the office. The Kalahari Typing School for Men had just been born: her first business, her own idea. She was certain that the men would come and the money would come with them. She couldn't wait to tell Mma Ramotswe.

◆

Mr Molefelo sat on a rock, under the empty sky, and told Mma Ramotswe what he had done all those years ago.

'I came to Gaborone when I was eighteen, to study at the Botswana College of Engineering. My family did not have much money but the government helped me with some of the costs. I stayed with a family in Gaborone and they were very kind to me and treated me like one of the family. The lady of the house was Mma Tsolamosese and she looked after me very well. Her husband worked at the prison.

★ *qwertyuiop*: the top line of letters on a computer or typewriter keyboard

'While I was a student, I met a girl and we went together to dances at the College. I was happy and proud to have such a lovely girlfriend. She was hoping to become a nurse and she had passed almost all the examinations she would need to start her training. Then one day she came to me with bad news. She was expecting a baby, she said, and I was the father. I was shocked, because I was only a student and I could not be a father to a baby yet.

'That night at Mma Tsolamosese's house, I could not sleep. I was very worried about the baby and could not think what to do. The next day my girlfriend said that soon she would have to tell her parents, and her father would probably come and kill me. This only made me feel worse. I thought I would have to leave the College and find work a long way from Gaborone, where he could not find me.

'My girlfriend was now becoming angry with me. She shouted at me and said that because of me she would have to try to get rid of the baby before it was born. She knew of an old woman to go to, but because it was illegal it would cost one hundred pula. This was a lot of money in those days.

'I went back to my room and thought about how I could get the money. Then I heard Mma Tsolamosese in the room next door. She turned on her radio. I knew it was a very expensive radio and I decided to steal it. Later that night I took it from the house and hid it in the garden. Then I opened one of the windows so that they would think a thief had come to the house. The next morning they discovered the open window and the missing radio. The police came, but said there was nothing they could do. They told Mma Tsolamosese that she would probably not get the radio back. Then after some days I went to the place where it was hidden and I took it into town. I sold it for one hundred pula.

'I gave my girlfriend the money and she cried and cried. She said she would go to the old woman at the weekend and she would meet me at our usual place after that. But I didn't go, Mma Ramotswe. I left her waiting there. And later, when she came to the house to see me, I was angry with her. She said she still loved me, but I told her I did not love her, and I pushed her away.

'There is not much more to say, Mma. After a few weeks I forgot all about it. I sometimes thought of the radio, and I felt cold inside, but I never thought of the girl. After I left College, I was too busy with my job to think much about my past. I have been lucky – I found a good wife and had two fine sons and three daughters. And I did well in business. Everything in my life was good until the day the ostrich thieves came to my farm and I started to think about the past. Now I want to make good the bad things I did.'

Mma Ramotswe stared at Mr Molefelo. He was telling the truth, she knew, because the truth was in his eyes.

'That was not easy to say. You have been very brave,' she said. 'And now? What do you want me to do now? I cannot change the past. I cannot take you back all those years.'

'It might be possible to do something,' he said. 'I would like to pay the Tsolamosese family back. I would like to give some money to the girl. And I would like to apologise to them. But I need your help to find them.'

'I will help you. I will try to find them,' said Mma Ramotswe, getting up and brushing the dust off her dress. 'Now, it is time for us to walk back. And on the way I shall tell you about a little problem I have with a small boy who killed a bird. You are a father, and maybe you can give me some advice.'

♦

Mr JLB Matekoni had told Charlie, the apprentice, to help Mma Makutsi fetch the typewriters from the Botswana Secretarial College.

'All the students here are girls, are they not, Mma?' he asked, as they walked together through the College.

'Yes,' she replied. 'There is no reason why that should be, but that is how it was in my day.'

'I would like to study here, then,' said the apprentice. 'I should like to sit in a classroom with all those girls.'

Mma Makutsi smiled. 'Some of them would like that too, I think. The wrong sort of girls.'

'There are no wrong sorts of girls,' Charlie replied. 'All girls have their uses. All are welcome.'

They reached the College office, and a pretty young secretary showed Mma Makutsi into the Assistant Principal's room while the apprentice sat on the edge of the secretary's desk.

Mma Manapotsi greeted Mma Makutsi warmly. 'It sounds very important being an assistant detective and assistant manager,' she said. 'I hope they are paying you what you deserve.'

'They are paying me as much as they can,' replied Mma Makutsi. 'Very few people get paid what they really deserve, even the President. I think we should pay him more.'

'Perhaps,' said Mma Manapotsi. 'I have always thought that the assistant principals of colleges should be paid more too. But we must not complain, must we, Mma? If everybody complained all the time, there would be no time for anything except complaints. We do not complain here at the Botswana Secretarial College. We get on with the job.'

The conversation continued in this way for a few minutes. From behind the door to the outside office came the sound of voices and occasional laughter.

'Now, let us fetch those typewriters.' said Mma Manapotsi. 'Your young man can carry them for you, if he is not too busy with that girl of mine.'

They went to a large cupboard, where the old typewriters were kept.

'They are very old,' said Mma Manapotsi. 'but most of them

could probably be made to work. They will need oiling.'

'There is plenty of oil in the garage,' said the apprentice, running his hand over the keyboard of one of the typewriters.

'But remember,' said Mma Manapotsi, 'these machines are not like cars. You will have to be more careful.'

They returned to Tlokweng Road Speedy Motors, where Mr JLB Matekoni had agreed the typewriters could be kept and worked on until Mma Makutsi had found a place for the classes to be held. Mma Ramotswe had offered to pay for an advertisement in the newspaper and Motholeli said she would like to help with the work on the typewriters.

'She is very interested in machines and is good with her hands,' said Mma Ramotswe.

'This business will be a great success,' said Mr JLB Matekoni.

Mma Makutsi was very pleased by his enthusiasm.

'Do you really think so, Rra?' she asked.

'I have no doubt of it,' said Mr JLB Matekoni.

Chapter 5   Getting Started

Mr Molefelo had given Mma Ramotswe very little information, so it was difficult to start her search. She knew that Mr Tsolamosese had been an officer at the prison, and the family had lived in a government house near the old airport. She also knew that the girlfriend's name was Tebogo Bathopi, that she came from Molepolole and was hoping to become a nurse. But that was twenty years ago. Tebogo had probably married and changed her name. When Mr Tsolamosese finished working at the prison, the Tsolamosese family had probably left their house. But it was hard to disappear completely in Botswana. There were fewer than two million people in the country, and even in Gaborone it was very difficult to be anonymous. Mr Tsolamosese was certainly too old to be working at the prison still. But somebody there might know where the family was now, so she decided to start her investigation with a telephone call to the prison.

The person answering the call did not know the name Tsolamosese, so she asked to speak to the oldest person in the office. There was a silence at the end of the phone while the oldest official was fetched.

'I am fifty-eight, Mma,' he said. 'Is that old enough, or do you want somebody of eighty or ninety?'

'Fifty-eight is very good, Rra,' she said. 'I would like to know if you remember Mr Tsolamosese. He worked in the prison some years ago. Perhaps he no longer works there.'

'Ah, yes. I was here when he worked here. I am sorry to tell you that he is late.'

Mma Ramotswe's heart sank. But perhaps Mma Tsolamosese was still alive and Mr Molefelo would still be able to put things right with her.

'And the widow?' she asked.

'She went away. Probably back to her village. You could ask the pensions people, of course,' said the voice. 'She will get her widow's pension all the time she is alive, and they will have her address.'

Mma Ramotswe knew the government pensions office, and she decided that a visit would be better than a phone call. The office would probably say they could not tell her the address, but there were ways round this. She went there immediately.

'I am looking for the widow of a government pensioner,' she said to the man behind the Enquiries desk. She gave him a piece of paper with Mr Tsolamosese's name on it. Underneath she had written 'Prisons Department', and after that the date of his death. The man went into the back office and looked through some papers.

29

'Yes,' he said. 'There is a widow of that name.'

Mma Ramotswe smiled. 'Thank you, Rra. Could you give me her address? I have something to deliver to her.'

The man shook his head. 'No, I cannot do that. It is not possible to give anyone that information.'

Mma Ramotswe took a deep breath.

'I would never tell you your job – a clever man like you does not need to be told by a woman how to do his job – but I think you have not understood the rule,' she said. 'The rule says you must not give the *name* of a pensioner. It says nothing about the address.'

'I do not think you are right, Mma. I know the rules. You are just the public.'

'Sometimes,' Mma Ramotswe continued, 'when there are so many rules, you can get them mixed up. You are thinking of Rule 25. This rule is really Rule 24 (b), part (i). The rule about addresses was Rule 18, which doesn't exists now.'

The man felt uncomfortable. Did rules have numbers? Nobody had told him, but it was possible.

'How do you know about these rules?' he asked.

'Have you not read the *Government Report*, Rra?' asked Mma Ramotswe. 'The rules are printed in the *Report* for everyone to see because they are there to protect the public. That is important.'

The man was now very unsure of himself.

'Of course,' continued Mma Ramotswe, 'if you are not able to help me, we must ask somebody else. Maybe you have a colleague who understands the rules better.'

'It is not necessary,' said the man. 'I was just waiting to see if you knew the rules. My job would be a lot easier if more people understood the rules. Now, I'll write down that address for you. It's a small village on the way to Lobatse. She is living there.'

Mma Ramotswe took the piece of paper from the man and

thanked him. As she left the office, she could not help smiling.

♦

Mma Makutsi was also searching. She was not looking for a person, but a place – somewhere she could open the Kalahari Typing School for Men. The younger apprentice had a good idea.

'There is a room at the back of the church,' he said. 'It is never used during the week and there are plenty of tables and chairs you could use. I will speak to the minister about it.'

The minister was happy to help, and the ten working typewriters were taken to the room and locked away in two cupboards. A small advertisement was put into the *Botswana Daily News* with the telephone number of the No.1 Ladies' Detective Agency.

On the day the advertisement appeared, Mma Makutsi bought a newspaper and arrived at work earlier than usual. It gave her great pleasure to see her name in print. 'That's me,' she thought. 'That's my name, in the newspaper.'

The first call came half an hour later, and many more followed during the day. By four o'clock there were twenty-two definite bookings for a place in the class. Ten would start that week, another ten would take the second course two months later, and two were placed on a waiting list.

'I told you it would work,' said Mr JLB Matekoni. 'I told you.'

♦

The first class took place on a Wednesday evening. Mma Makutsi had taken some time to arrange the desks and put exercise papers on each one. At the front of the room she had put a blackboard, with a drawing of the keyboard on it. Her method of teaching would be the same as the Botswana Secretarial College; every finger must be taught to know its place. The students would learn by repeating and practising exercises.

The class was supposed to begin at six, but most of her students were there before then. Mma Makutsi checked her watch, counted the students, and said that class would begin.

The hour went very quickly. The students were told about the different parts of the typewriter, then they were asked to type, all together, the word *hat*.

'Now,' called out Mma Makutsi, '*h* and *a* and *t*. Now stop.'

A hand went up.

'My *h* does not work, Mma', said a smartly-dressed man. 'I pressed it twice but it has not worked. I have typed *at*.'

Mma Makutsi was prepared for this. 'Some keys are not in working order,' she said. 'This does not matter. You must still press them, because you will find that these keys will work in your office. It does not matter at this stage.'

She looked at the man, who had carefully cut hair and a small moustache. He smiled at her, and they moved on to new words.

'Cat,' shouted Mma Makutsi. 'And sat. Hat, cat, fat.'

At the end of the hour, Mma Makutsi went round the desks and looked at the students' work. She had a good word for everyone – something she had learnt the value of at the Botswana Secretarial College.

'You will be a very good typist, Rra,' she said to one man, and 'You have very good finger control,' to another. To the man with the moustache she said, 'You have typed *cat* very clearly. That is very good.'

When the class was over the men left the church room, talking together. Mma Makutsi heard one man say to another, 'She is a good teacher, that woman. She does not make me feel stupid. She is good at her job.'

Alone in the room, she smiled to herself. She had enjoyed the class, and discovered that she had the ability to teach. And in addition, in the small cash box on her desk was the money the men had paid for their first lesson – this was her money to use as she wished. She planned to give a small amount to Mma Ramotswe for the cost of the telephone calls, but the rest would go into the bank. Better days, she was sure, lay ahead.

Chapter 6 Making Progress

Mma Ramotswe drove down the Lobatse road in her little white van, with the morning sun shining through the open window. There was not much traffic on the road; an occasional van or crowded bus, one or two army vehicles and a few private cars. Lobatse was a little over an hour's drive, and there was just enough activity on the way to stop her feeling bored.

A journey was a good time to think, and as she drove Mma Ramotswe thought about some possible endings for this rather unusual case. The more she thought about Mr Molefelo, the more she admired him. Most people forget about really old wrongs, sometimes on purpose, sometimes just by allowing the past to quietly disappear on its own. But Mr Molefelo had remembered, and then decided to do something about it.

It was difficult to imagine what Mma Tsolamosese would say when she heard the truth about what had happened all those years ago. She would certainly be angry. She might even talk of going to the police. Mr Molefelo had probably not thought of that possibility when he came to Mma Ramotswe. He was expecting to put things right informally, but the situation might be different if the police were asked to investigate.

Mma Ramotswe hoped that Mma Tsolamosese would not want to go to the police. She hoped that she could tell Mr Molefelo to apologise and to buy her a new radio. He had said that money was not a problem. 'I shall pay whatever is necessary,' he had said. 'It's easy to get money out of the bank, but you can't get peace of mind out of a bank.'

The turning to the village was close and, if her directions were correct, Mma Tsolamosese's house was at the edge of the village. She found it without a problem.

An old woman was sitting on a chair outside the house. She stood up as Mma Ramotswe got out of her little white van, and they exchanged greetings in the traditional way. Mma Ramotswe introduced herself and asked if the woman was Mma Tsolamosese. The woman smiled. She had a pleasant, open face and Mma Ramotswe liked her immediately.

Mma Ramotswe accepted the invitation to sit down and Mma Tsolamosese fetched some water for her from the house. From inside the house came the sound of children's voices.

'There are two children living here,' said Mma Tsolamosese. 'There is the daughter of one of my sons, whose wife has gone to look after her mother in Shashe. Then there is the daughter of my daughter, who is late. I am looking after both children.'

Mma Tsolamosese looked very carefully at Mma Ramotswe, at her face and clothes. 'I am very happy to see you, Mma, but I wonder why you have come,' she said.

'I have come to talk to you about something that happened a long time ago,' said Mma Ramotswe. 'I believe your late husband worked for the Prison Department,' she continued. 'And you lived near the old air field in Gaborone? And you let students live in one of your rooms?'

'We always did that,' said Mma Tsolamosese. 'The money helped, although they could not afford much.'

'There was a student called Molefelo. He was studying at the Botswana College of Engineering. Do you remember him?'

Mma Tsolamosese smiled. 'I remember that boy very well. He was a very nice boy. He was always clean.'

Mma Ramotswe paused. It was not going to be easy to tell her, even now, after all this time. But it was part of her job to

'I am very happy to see you, Mma, but I wonder why you have come.'

tell people bad news, and she had to do it.

'When he was staying with you, somebody stole a radio from your house. Did that happen?'

'Yes, it did happen. It was a very fine radio.'

Mma Ramotswe took a deep breath. 'Molefelo took it,' she said. 'He stole the radio.'

At first, Mma Tsolamosese looked confused. 'No,' she said. 'He did not do it. He was living with us at the time. It was probably one of the prisoners. That is always a danger when you live near a prison.'

'No, Mma,' said Mma Ramotswe, gently. 'It was Molefelo. He needed money urgently for ... for something he had to do. So he stole the radio and left a window open so you thought a thief had come into the house. He sold it for one hundred pula. That is the truth.'

Mma Tsolamosese looked up sharply. 'How do you know this, Mma? You weren't there.'

'He told me himself. He has felt bad about it for years – and now he wants to come and apologise. He wants to buy you a new radio. He wants to put things right.'

'I do not want a radio,' said Mma Tsolamosese. 'I do not like the music they play now.'

'It is important to him,' said Mma Ramotswe. 'Have you ever done anything bad yourself, Mma?' she asked. 'And do you remember wanting to put right a bad thing you have done?'

There was a silence between them.

'Yes, I remember that.'

Mma Ramotswe lost no time. 'Well, that is how Molefelo feels now. Should you not give him the chance to say sorry?'

Mma Tsolamosese was quiet for a moment. 'Yes,' she said. 'It was a long time ago. It is good that he is thinking this now. I would not like him to suffer in his heart.'

They sat together in the sunlight. There were vegetables to

prepare, and Mma Ramotswe helped with this. They drank tea and felt comfortable together. Mma Tsolamosese agreed that Mma Ramotswe should bring Molefelo to the village so they could meet.

'He was just a young boy when those things happened,' said Mma Tsolamosese.

'Yes, he is a different person now,' said Mma Ramotswe.

A young teenage girl came out of the house.

'This is the daughter of my son. She is very helpful with the little one,' said Mma Tsolamosese. She smiled at the child. 'Bring her out to see Mma.'

The girl went back into the house and returned with a child of about two.

'This is the child of my late daughter. I am looking after her.'

Mma Ramotswe took the child's hand in her own. 'She is a very pretty child, Mma. She will grow into a beautiful lady in time,' she said.

Mma Tsolamosese turned her head away, and Mma Ramotswe saw that she was upset, although she did not understand why.

'Take her in now, Koketso. I think she might be hungry,' Mma Tsolamosese said to the teenage girl.

They sat in silence for a few moments after the children had gone.

'I am sorry if I upset you,' said Mma Ramotswe. 'I did not mean to.'

'It is not your fault, Mma. You did not know.' Mma Tsolamosese sounded tired. 'That child ... her mother, who is late, had that disease which has run this way and that through the country, and everywhere. That is how she died. And the child ...'

Mma Ramotswe knew what was coming next.

'The doctor said that the child will become ill too. She will not live. That is why I was upset,' Mma Tsolamosese explained. 'You did not mean it, but you were talking about something that will never be.'

Mma Ramotswe pushed the bowl of vegetables to one side and went over to Mma Tsolamosese. She put an arm around her shoulder.

'I am sorry, Mma,' she said. 'I am very sorry.'

There was nothing more to say, but as she stood there, the idea came to Mma Ramotswe of what Mr Molefelo could do.

♦

The students of the Kalahari Typing School for Men met at the church room every weekday night, except for Fridays. They made such good progress that Mma Makutsi realised they could complete their course in five weeks instead of six.

'It will be the same course,' she told them, 'but you people will finish it one week early.'

'Will we get some money back?' asked one of the men, and this caused a little laughter from the others.

'No,' said Mma Makutsi. 'Certainly not.' She had expected something like this and had her answer ready. 'You will get the same amount of knowledge. So that costs the same amount of money. That is fair.'

They accepted her reply without complaint, and she moved quickly on to their next exercise. To give them a change from copy-typing, they were all invited to write a short essay in the last half hour of the class. They were not expected to write more than about half a page, but they should try to do this with as few mistakes as possible. There would be fifty points for a perfect essay, with two marks taken off for each mistake. The title, she said, was 'The Important Things in My Life', and the essay should be written anonymously. In this way nobody would feel embarrassed: people could write about the things that really mattered to them without feeling shy.

The students started typing enthusiastically. At the end of the class the essays were all left on the table. Mma Makutsi intended to take them home and read them there, but a quick look at the one on the top of the pile interested her so much that she sat down and read through them immediately. All of life was there: mothers, wives, sport, success at work, motor cars; everything that men liked. There was an essay about one man's young son and a couple about the local Zebras football team.

Then, almost at the bottom of the pile, she found this: 'I have discovered something very important in my life. I did not expect to find it, but it came to me suddenly, like lightning. My life has not been very exciting until now, but for a week my heart has been racing. It is a lady I have met. She is one of the most beautiful ladies I have ever seen, and I think that she must be one of the kindest, nicest ladies in Botswana. She always smiles at me and does not mind if I make mistakes. She has walked past me and has made my heart sing, although she does not know it. I do not know whether to tell her that she is filling my head with ideas of love. If I tell her, she might say I am not good enough for her. But if I do not tell her, then she may never know how I feel. She is the most important thing in my life. I cannot stop thinking of her, even when she is teaching me typing.'

Mma Makutsi stared at the essay in great surprise. One of her students, one of these men, was in love with her! Of course, there was no name on the essay, but she was in no doubt about the writer. At first, she had been so interested in the sense of it that she was not thinking about the typing. Now, as she looked again, she saw that every letter h was missing. The last sentence read: 'I cannot stop t inking of er.'

Her heart was beating with excitement. Mma Makutsi took out a pencil and wrote at the bottom of the essay: 'This is a very well-typed essay. You should tell this lady, though, or she might never know. You should ask her to go out with you after the class. That is what you should do.'

Chapter 7 One Good Man, and then Another

Mma Silvia Potokwani was the matron of the orphan farm, which was twenty minutes' drive to the east of the town. She had worked there for fifteen years and it was said that she remembered the name of every orphan who had stayed at the farm during that time. She also knew a lot of important people in Botswana and she remembered them all for the ways they could help the orphan farm. Most people were not brave enough to refuse her requests, so the orphan children usually had everything they needed.

Mr JLB Matekoni had known Mma Potokwani for over twenty years and was called out regularly to attend to mechanical problems. He kept alive their old van, and he also looked after the water pump. It was time to buy a new pump but Mr JLB Matekoni knew that Mma Potokwani would not agree to this. She believed it was still possible to keep the pump working, so it was a waste, in her opinion, to get rid of it.

Mr JLB Matekoni and Mma Ramotswe drove to the orphan farm together and left his van under a tree in front of the office. Mma Potokwani saw them from the window and went out to greet them.

'My two very good friends,' she said, 'both arriving at the same time! It is very good to see you.'

'He is my driver now,' joked Mma Ramotswe. 'I do not have to drive now.'

'And I don't have to cook,' added Mr JLB Matekoni.

'But you never did cook, Rra,' said Mma Potokwani.

'I sometimes cooked,' said Mr JLB Matekoni.

'When did you cook?' asked Mma Potokwani.

'Sometimes,' said Mr JLB Matekoni. 'But we must not stand around and talk about cooking. I must go and fix this pump. What is it doing now?'

Mma Potokwani explained about the strange noises the pump was making.

'Sometimes it sounds like an animal calling out to its baby. And it is shaking like a dog too. That is what it is doing.'

'It is a very old pump,' said Mr JLB Matekoni. 'Machines don't last for ever, you know. Just like us, they have to die sometime.'

But he could tell that Mma Potokwani did not want to hear this.

'It may be old,' she said, 'but it is still working, isn't it? If I have to buy a new pump, that will take money I could use for other things. The children need shoes. They need clothes. I have to pay the cooks and everybody. There is no money for new pumps.'

'I was only explaining the truth about machines. I did not say I would not try to fix it.'

'Good,' said Mma Potokwani. 'Now,' she said, turning to Mma Ramotswe, 'while Mr JLB Matekoni is fixing the pump we shall have tea. And when he has finished, his tea will be ready and we will keep a large piece of fruit cake for him.'

♦

Mr JLB Matekoni had to walk across a large field to reach the pump house. There was water under ground; sweet, fresh water that the pump brought up for the orphan farm to use. He entered the pump house, taking care to look out for snakes, which liked to lie in such places. At first the pump seemed to be working normally. But as he looked at it, there was suddenly another sound and it was just as Mma Potokwani had described. It sounded like an animal calling to its baby. But to Mr JLB Matekoni's ears it meant something different; it was the sound of a dying pump.

He switched the pump off and opened his tool box. Now there was silence. He felt tired. He closed his tool box again and made a decision. He would not fix this pump again. The time had come to tell Mma Potokwani that *he* was the mechanic, not her. He knew when a pump had come to the end of its life. She would have to listen to him this time. He would say: 'Mma Potokwani, I have examined the pump and it cannot be fixed. You must telephone one of the rich people you know and tell them that a new pump is needed.'

He closed the door behind him and walked back across the field.

♦

'This is very good cake,' said Mma Ramotswe. 'You must tell me how to make it. Motholeli and Puso would like it.'

Mma Potokwani smiled as she remembered the children. 'I hope they are doing well,' she said.

'We are happy to have them,' said Mma Ramotswe. 'They can live with us until they are grown up. Motholeli wants to be a mechanic – did you know that? She is very good with machines and Mr JLB Matekoni is going to teach her.'

Mma Potokwani was pleased to hear this. 'And her brother?' she said. 'Is he also doing well?'

Mma Ramotswe paused. 'He is eating well and he is growing. Already I have bought him new shoes. There is nothing wrong there, it's just that …'

'Behaviour?' suggested Mma Potokwani.

'Yes,' agreed Mma Ramotswe. 'I thought you might be able to advise me. You know all about children.'

Mma Ramotswe described some of the things that had happened, including the day Puso killed the bird with a catapult.

'He didn't learn that here,' said Mma Potokwani.

'And he told Mr JLB Matekoni he hated him,' Mma Ramotswe continued. 'It makes me think that somebody has poured poison into his ear.'

'That is probably truer than you think, Mma,' said Mma

Potokwani. 'He goes to school now, doesn't he? He is learning things from other children, and some of those children are bad. They are the ones with the poison.' She poured them both more tea. 'And he will know he is different from the other boys because he's an orphan, but he will have no understanding of his situation, or that you are now his family. So he's blaming you because he's lost.'

Mma Ramotswe thought this sounded sensible, but what could they do? They had tried to be kind, and had given him more attention, but that didn't seem to help.

'I think,' said Mma Potokwani, 'that it is time for Mr JLB Matekoni to start giving him some rules to live by. Other boys have fathers or uncles to do that. He needs to be more of a father to Puso, and to be stronger. He is such a kind, gentle man – we all know that – but maybe that is not what that little boy needs.'

Mma Ramotswe thought about this. 'So, Mr JLB Matekoni should be stricter with Puso?'

Mma Potokwani smiled. 'A little. But he really needs to do things with Puso – take the boy out with him in his van, or to watch the older boys playing football. Things like that.'

'I shall tell him,' said Mma Ramotswe.

♦

'You were very brave back there,' said Mma Ramotswe to Mr JLB Matekoni, as they travelled back from the orphan farm. 'It is not easy to tell Mma Potokwani something she does not want to hear, but you did it.'

'I did not think I could do it, but when I looked at that old pump, and heard the strange noises it was making, I just decided I could not fix it again,' replied Mr JLB Matekoni. 'There is a time to let a machine go. But she will find someone to pay for the new pump,' he continued. 'Already she was thinking about who to telephone.'

He had not left without doing something positive; there were problems with the old van that the orphan farm used to take the children out, and he was able to do the repairs. In time, this would also need to go, but now he could still manage to keep it on the road.

Mma Ramotswe decided this was a good time to talk about Puso's behaviour.

'Mma Potokwani was not surprised to hear about Puso,' she began. 'She said that boys are often difficult. She said that men need to spend time with boys, to help them. If not, boys can be confused and difficult. She suggested that if you did more with Puso, then he would think of you more as his father.'

Mr JLB Matekoni looked upset. 'She must think that I am not a good father.'

'Not at all,' said Mma Ramotswe. 'Mma Potokwani said that you were the best father a boy could have.'

This was not true, but it was close to the truth. Perhaps she hadn't said it, but Mma Ramotswe was sure that she meant it.

Mr JLB Matekoni was pleased to hear it. 'That was a kind thing for her to say,' he said. 'I shall try to do more with him, as she suggested. I shall take him out in the van.'

'Good idea,' said Mma Ramotswe. 'And you could play games with him. Football, perhaps.'

When they returned to Zebra Drive, while Mma Ramotswe prepared the evening meal, Mr JLB Matekoni took Puso for a ride in his van. On the way home, they stopped at a café for potato chips, which they ate in the van. Then they drove home, and Mma Ramotswe saw that they were both smiling.

♦

The next day, at the shared offices of the No.1 Ladies' Detective Agency and Tlokweng Road Speedy Motors there was a feeling of happiness in the air. Mr JLB Matekoni was happy about the pump situation at the orphan farm, and the change in his relationship with Puso. Mma Ramotswe was also happy about this, and when cheques arrived from three of her clients her mood was even more cheerful. And there was something different about Mma Makutsi. Mma Ramotswe noticed that she was wearing a new dress and shoes, but it was more than that.

'You are happy today, Mma,' she said.

'It is a nice day and we have received those cheques,' replied Mma Makutsi.

'Yes, but there is something more, isn't there?'

'You're the detective,' said Mma Makutsi, smiling. 'You tell me what it is.'

'You have met a man,' said Mma Ramotswe. 'I hope he is a nice man.'

'Oh, he is,' said Mma Makutsi, happily. 'He is a very handsome man, with a moustache. He has a nice smile too.'

'And have you been out dancing with him? Men with moustaches can be good dancers.'

'We haven't actually been out together yet,' Mma Makutsi said. 'But that will happen soon. Maybe tonight.'

♦

Mr Bernard Selelipeng was the first student to arrive that evening, twenty minutes before the class started. Mma Makutsi was already there, putting out the papers for the evening's exercises.

She smiled at him, and he went over to his desk. His essay was already on it. He picked it up and began to read the writing at the bottom of the page. He looked up, and she knew immediately that she had done the right thing. He walked across the room to stand in front of her.

'I wanted to write the truth,' he said, 'and that was the truth.

Your reply is just what I was hoping for. I would like to ask you to come for a drink with me after the class tonight. Will you be free?'

Mma Makutsi accepted his invitation, and for the rest of the class she could think of nothing else. After the other students had left, Mma Makutsi and Bernard Selelipeng walked together to his car, and drove to a bar on the edge of town.

It was an expensive place, and there was music playing in the background as they went in. A waiter appeared immediately to take their order. Bernard Selelipeng ordered a beer, and Mma Makutsi, who never drank alcohol, ordered a fruit juice.

Bernard Selelipeng knocked his glass gently against hers and smiled. His smile, she thought, was the most attractive thing about him. They had not made much conversation in the car, and now he asked her where she lived and what her job was during the day. Mma Makutsi was not sure whether to tell him about the No.1 Ladies' Detective Agency. She was not certain how he would feel about her being a detective, even if only an assistant detective. So she just told him she was Assistant Manager of Tlokweng Road Speedy Motors.

'And what about you, Rra? What do you do?'

'I work in the diamond office,' he said. 'I am a manager there.'

Mma Makutsi wondered why such a handsome man, with a good job, a car and of an interesting age, was unmarried. She looked at his left hand as he lifted the glass of beer to his mouth. There was no ring on it.

'I live alone,' said Bernard Selelipeng, 'I have one of the new apartments at the edge of the town. Near your garage.'

'They are very nice apartments,' said Mma Makutsi. 'But why do you live alone? Most people would get lonely.'

'I am divorced,' said Bernard Selelipeng. 'My wife went away with another man and took our children with her. That is why

46

'I would like to ask you to come for a drink with me after the class tonight.'

I am alone.'

Mma Makutsi was very surprised that a woman could leave a man like this. She could only imagine that his wife had met a richer, more successful man.

They made conversation for several hours. He was entertaining and funny, and she laughed at his descriptions of some of his colleagues at the diamond office. She told him about the apprentices, and he laughed at them. Then, just before ten o'clock, he looked at his watch and said that he would be happy to take her home. He had a meeting early the following morning and did not want to be too late.

Outside her house he touched her gently on the shoulder and said goodnight.

'I will see you at the class tomorrow,' he said, and added, 'I cannot wait for us to go out again. There is a film I would like to see at the cinema. Perhaps we can go to that.'

'I would like that very much,' said Mma Makutsi.

She watched him drive down the road, the red lights of his car disappearing into the night. He was so kind, such a gentleman. How fortunate, she thought, that she and Mma Ramotswe had both found such good men, when everyone knew there were so many bad men about.

Chapter 8 An Unhappy Client

Mma Ramotswe and Mma Makutsi had almost forgotten about the Satisfaction Guaranteed Detective Agency, but then two things happened to remind them. The first was an interview in the local newspaper. It covered a whole page, and at the top there was a picture of Mr Buthelezi sitting behind his desk. In one hand he was holding a cigarette and in the other was the telephone. Mma Ramotswe had seen the newspaper first, and was now in the office reading it to Mma Makutsi.

'From New York and Johannesburg to Gaborone,' she read. 'We spoke to Mr Buthelezi and asked him what it was like to be a private detective in Gaborone. "It is quite hard being the first real detective," he said. "There are, as people know, one or two ladies who have been doing a little work like this and there will always be a few jobs they can do. Cases connected with children, for example. But for the real work, you need a real detective."'

Mma Ramotswe looked across at Mma Makutsi, who was drinking her bush tea slowly and thoughtfully. She looked back at the newspaper and continued reading.

'"I have had plenty of experience. I worked with the CID in Johannesburg on many different cases. It was very hard there and I learnt how thieves and murderers think. You have to be strong in this business. That's why men are best at it. They're stronger than women.

'"I have been very busy since I opened my business in Gaborone. It is clear that there are many problems in this city, so if any readers have something that needs investigating, I am their man. I repeat, I am their man. You ask me, what are the best qualities for a private detective? First, you have to understand the human mind. You have to know why people do the things they do. Then you need a good eye for detail. We have to notice things – often very little things – so we can learn the truth for our clients. So a private detective is like a camera, always taking photographs in his mind and always trying to understand what is happening. That is the secret.

'"You ask, how can you become a private detective? You have to learn the job, in the CID. You cannot just put up a sign and say you are a private detective. And it helps if you've been to London or New York, or somewhere like that, because then you know the world and nobody will be able to make a fool of

49

you. I have worked in New York. Some of the detectives there were my close friends.

"'But now I'm back in my home town. I know a lot, and I can find out anything I don't know. Give me a call. Any time!'"

Mma Ramotswe finished reading and threw the newspaper down angrily. Mr Buthelezi had said some things about women, and women detectives, which were clearly aimed at her, and she should reply. But he probably wanted an answer, as this would give even more attention to his business. She thought too that there were possibly a lot of readers with the same opinion; that men were better at the job than women.

'I'm going to ask Charlie for his opinion,' she said to Mma Makutsi. 'Could you go and fetch him please?'

The apprentice came to the office, and was asked to read the newspaper. When he had finished, he handed it back to Mma Ramotswe.

'I am sorry, Mma,' he said. 'This is going to make it difficult for your business. Everyone will go to this man now. He has worked in Johannesburg – and New York! He is a very clever man. But I do not want the business to go to him, so I am very sorry.'

After he had left the room Mma Makutsi said, 'That boy is stupid. We all know he only cares about girls and cars. Don't believe anything he says.'

'He's not so stupid,' said Mma Ramotswe. 'He had to pass some exams to become an apprentice. But I think many people will think the same as him, and we cannot change that.'

◆

Later that afternoon, when Mma Makutsi was out of the office checking something for a client, a lady visited the detective agency. She arrived in a shiny new car. She was in her late thirties, maybe a little younger than Mma Ramotswe. She was dressed very well, in expensive clothes. Mma Ramotswe thought she was perhaps a businesswoman, or that she worked for the government in a well-paid job.

The woman did not give her name. 'I must tell you,' she said, 'that I have no confidence in private detectives. I don't mean to be rude, but I have just had an unpleasant experience with another detective agency.'

Mma Ramotswe understood. 'The Satisfaction Guaranteed Agency?' she asked.

'Yes,' said the woman. 'That man! I do not know how he can call himself a private detective.'

Mma Ramotswe wished that Mma Makutsi was there to share this moment. Then it suddenly came to her that she should make an offer to her visitor. It would be the right thing to do.

'Before you continue, Mma,' she began, 'I must say one thing. If you have suffered at the hands of someone else in my profession – and I am not surprised to hear it – then the No.1 Ladies' Detective Agency will complete the enquiry for you.'

The woman was surprised and pleased.

'You are very good, Mma.' She said. 'I did not come expecting that, but I am happy to accept your offer. I can tell that things are different in this place.'

'They are,' said Mma Ramotswe. 'We do not make promises we cannot keep. We are not like that.'

'Good. Then let me tell you what happened.'

She had gone to see Mr Buthelezi after seeing his advertisement in the newspaper.

'I live in Mochudi,' she said. 'I am a doctor in the hospital there and I have four children all at school there. The problem is that my husband has a job in Gaborone and he did not like to drive in from Mochudi every morning and back again. So we bought a small apartment here.'

Mma Ramotswe guessed what was coming next, and she was

right. The woman said that she thought her husband was seeing another woman.

'I usually telephone him in the evenings. We talk about things that have happened during the day, and the children talk to their father. But now he is never in when I call. He says this is because he goes for a lot of walks, but I do not believe him.'

Mr Buthelezi had said he would follow the husband and tell her what he was doing.

'But I don't think he did,' she said. 'He says he followed him and that he is going to church. That is crazy. My husband does not go to church. I have tried to make him go, but he will not. When he came home last weekend I said to him on Sunday, "Let's go to church," but he said that he did not want to go. If he had suddenly become interested in the church, he would certainly want to go on a Sunday. That proves it, in my mind.'

Mma Ramotswe agreed.

'But there is something more. I paid Mr Buthelezi a lot of money when I first went to him. When I said I wanted some of it back, he refused. So I came to you.'

Mma Ramotswe smiled. 'I will do my best. I will find out what is happening and I will tell you all about it.'

They discussed the details, including the husband's name and the address of the place where he worked. The woman then gave Mma Ramotswe a photograph of her husband. He was very well dressed, smiling at the camera. He had carefully-cut hair and a moustache.

'This will be very useful, Mma Selelipeng,' said Mma Ramotswe. She looked at the photograph again. This was not a strong face, she thought. This Bernard Selelipeng probably only needed a reminder of his duties as a husband and father, and all would be well again. She was sure of it.

♦

At the same time that evening, Mma Makutsi's typing class was going very well. She had given the students a test, to find out their speed, and had been pleasantly surprised by the results. Mr Bernard Selelipeng had done very well, with the highest number of words typed in a minute.

After the class ended, they met outside the church and decided to go to the cinema first, then to a café afterwards.

The film was full of silly, rich people living in a world that was nothing like real life. Mma Makutsi was not very interested in it; her thoughts were with Mr Bernard Selelipeng. In the middle of the performance he put his hand into hers and she felt both happy and excited. Romantic thoughts filled her head and she closed her eyes with pleasure.

After the cinema they went to a café in the centre of town and ordered a meal. They sat at a table near the door, and held hands under the table. That is where they were when Mma Ramotswe and Mr JLB Matekoni came in. Mma Makutsi introduced her friend and Mma Ramotswe smiled and greeted him politely. But Mma Ramotswe and Mr JLB Matekoni did not stay long in the café.

'You are upset about something,' said Mr JLB Matekoni, as they returned to his van.

'I am very sad,' said Mma Ramotswe. 'I have found something out, but I am too upset to talk about it. Please drive me back to my house, Mr JLB Matekoni. I am very sad.'

Chapter 9 Finding Tebogo

Yes, thought Mma Ramotswe, the world could sometimes be very cruel. But there was no point in sitting and thinking about all the things that go wrong in life. There was much to be grateful for, and the ordinary things must still be done. And so she had to get back to work and do something about her client, Mr Molefelo.

It was over a week since she had found Mma Tsolamosese, and that had been the easy part. She now had to find the other person, Tebogo.

She did not have much information about her. She knew Tebogo had wanted to become a nurse, so she started her search with that. But there was nobody of her name listed in Botswana as a nurse. There was only one other thing that Mma Ramotswe knew about Tebogo; her home town was Molepolole. She decided to go there and try to find the family. Mma Ramotswe had some old friends there and it would be pleasant to visit them. One of her friends had lived in Molepolole for many years and knew everyone in the town, so she might have some information. Perhaps Tebogo herself lived there now, and she could visit her. She would have to be careful, especially if Tebogo was married. Her husband might not know about the baby.

It was a beautiful morning as Mma Ramotswe started on her journey to Molepolole. As she drove, she thought about her discovery in the café. She had been shocked to find Mma Makutsi with Mr Selelipeng, and the following morning in the office Mma Makutsi had talked a lot about him. She felt they made a very good couple.

'I did not tell you earlier because I wanted to be sure of him. I did not want to say that I had found the right man for me, then have to tell you one week later that it had ended,' she had said to her employer.

Mma Ramotswe had not been sure of what to do next. She could be honest and tell Mma Makutsi the truth about Mr Selelipeng immediately. But this seemed so cruel, and she thought there might be a way of doing something in the background that would make it a little easier.

Of course there was always the possibility that Mma Makutsi

knew all about his wife and family. Mma Ramotswe wondered if this was likely. Mma Makutsi did not have much time; soon younger men would not want her and then she would only be left with the possibility of an old man. Perhaps she did know about Mr Bernard Selelipeng's situation and did not care. But Mma Ramotswe remembered their recent conversation about the difficulty of meeting men in bars because they were all married. No, she thought, Mma Makutsi would not want to enter into a relationship with a married man, not even a handsome one with a moustache.

Mma Ramotswe put these thoughts to one side as she arrived in Molepolole. She drove first to the house of her old friend, Mma Ntombi Boko. After almost forty years working for the Botswana National Bank in Gaborone, Mma Boko had left her job and bought a house in Molepolole. Her days were now spent organising a club for local women, and because of this she knew everybody in town.

Mma Ramotswe found her friend at the side of the house, standing over a small brick oven. There was a large cooking pot on the top, and the sweet smell of jam was in the air.

Mma Boko's greeting was warm. 'Precious Ramotswe! Yes, it is you!'

'It is me,' said Mma Ramotswe. 'I have come to see you.'

'I am very glad,' said Mma Boko. 'I was sitting here making this jam and thinking, "Where is everybody today? Why has nobody come to talk to me?"'

'And then I arrived, just in time!'

Mma Ramotswe knew that Mma Boko loved to see her friends and hear all their news. For her, a day without the chance for a good conversation was very boring.

Mma Ramotswe took the small spoonful of jam which her friend offered her.

'It is good,' she said. 'This is the best jam in Botswana, I think.'

They sat down and talked. Mma Boko told Mma Ramotswe about her sixteen grandchildren. They were all clever, she said.

Mma Ramotswe told her about Mr JLB Matekoni's illness, and how both businesses now shared the same offices at Tlokweng Road Speedy Motors. She told her about the two orphan children, and the problems with Puso.

'Boys do go through difficult times like that,' said Mma Boko. 'It can last for fifty years.'

Then, after they had talked for some time, Mma Ramotswe asked Mma Boko about Tebogo.

'About twenty years ago this girl – she is a woman now – came to Gaborone from Molepolole to study nursing, but I do not think she finished her training. Something happened to her in Gaborone, which somebody now wants to put right. I cannot tell you what that thing was, but the other person is very serious about putting things right. But he does not know where this girl is and that is why I have come to you. I thought you could help me to find out where this woman is, if she is still alive.'

'Of course she is still alive,' said Mma Boko, laughing. 'She is now called Mma Tshenyogo.'

Mma Ramotswe was very pleased. She had not thought it would be so easy, but she had had a feeling that Mma Boko was the right person to ask. She had always thought the best way of finding information was to ask a woman who keeps her eyes and ears open and likes to talk. It was no use asking men; they were simply not interested enough in other people.

'And can you tell me where Tebogo is?'

'Over there,' answered Mma Boko, pointing across her garden to a neighbouring house. 'Just over there. Look, she is coming out of the house with one of the children – that girl, who is sixteen now. That is her first born, her first daughter.'

Mma Ramotswe looked across to the house. She saw a

woman coming out of the back door, with a girl in a yellow dress. There were chickens in the garden and the girl threw some food to them.

'She is a good person and a clever lady. She is also a wonderful cook and she keeps that house beautifully clean.'

'So she did not finish her nurses' training?' asked Mma Ramotswe.

'No, she is not a nurse, but maybe one of her daughters will study nursing,' said Mma Boko.

'I must go and see her,' said Mma Ramotswe. 'But first I have a present for you, in my van.'

She walked over to the van and came back with a package. Mma Boko took the brown paper off the package and saw that it was a length of printed cotton material, enough for a dress.

'You are very kind Mma,' she said. 'This will make a fine dress.'

'And you are a very useful friend,' said Mma Ramotswe. 'And now I must go and talk to that lady.'

♦

Mr Molefelo arrived at the No.1 Ladies' Detective Agency the following morning. He was very anxious to hear what Mma Ramotswe had found out, and could not wait any longer.

He was early for his appointment and waited outside in his car until exactly eleven o'clock. Mma Makutsi showed him into the office and then returned to her desk. Mr Molefelo greeted Mma Ramotswe and then looked at Mma Makutsi.

'I wonder, Mma …' he began.

Mma Ramotswe caught Mma Makutsi's eye, and it was enough for a message to pass between them.

'I have to go to the post, Mma,' said Mma Makutsi. 'Shall I go now?'

'A very good idea,' replied Mma Ramotswe.

Mma Makutsi left the office, and as soon as she had gone Mr Molefelo spoke.

'I must know, Mma. Are they late? Are they late?'

'No, they are not late, Rra,' said Mma Ramotswe. 'Mr Tsolamosese has died, but his widow is still alive. You came to me in time.'

Mr Molefelo was pleased to know this. 'So, I can do what I need to do.'

'I shall tell you first about Tebogo. She is well. She told me about her life,' said Mma Ramotswe. 'She did not become a nurse. She was very upset about the baby. She said that she cried for many months and had bad dreams about what she had done.'

'That was my fault,' said Mr Molefelo. 'It was wrong of me to say that she should end that baby. I know that.'

'She was upset about you too,' Mma Ramotswe continued. 'She said that she loved you and that you had told her that too. When you changed your mind, she was very upset. She said that you had a hard heart.'

Mr Molefelo looked down at the floor. 'It is true. I had a hard heart …'

'But then she met another boy and he asked her to marry him. They live out at Molepolole and they have been happy. They have five children. I met the oldest girl.'

Mr Molefelo listened carefully to Mma Ramotswe. 'Is that all that happened? Did you tell her how sorry I was?'

'I did,' said Mma Ramotswe. 'She said that you must not worry. Her life has been very good and she hopes that you have been happy too.' She paused. 'I think that you wanted to help her in some way, didn't you, Rra?'

Mr Molefelo smiled. 'Yes, and I meant it. I want to give her some money.'

'That might not be the best way to do it. What do you think her husband will think if she receives money from an old

'I shall tell you first about Tebogo.'

boyfriend? He might not like it at all.'

'Then what can I do?'

'I met her daughter,' said Mma Ramotswe. 'She is a clever girl and she would like to be a nurse. But there are few places for training. Only the girls with the best exam results will get the opportunity. She will have a better chance if she goes for a year or two to a private school.'

'That costs a lot of money,' said Mr Molefelo.

'I do not think you can put things right cheaply, Rra. Do you?' said Mma Ramotswe.

Mr Molefelo paused, and then smiled. 'I think you are right. I will pay for that girl to go to a good school here in Gaborone.'

'That's half the medicine,' thought Mma Ramotswe. She looked out of the window for the apprentice. He was not there yet, but he should be back very soon. While they were waiting, she told Mr Molefelo how she had found Mma Tsolamosese.

'Was she very angry with me?'

'She was very surprised and at first she did not believe that you had done it. Then she said that she thought you were very brave to tell what had happened.'

Mr Molefelo looked sad. 'She must think I am very bad,' he said.

'She is an old woman. She understands that young men can behave like that,' said Mma Ramotswe. 'She is not angry with you, and she is happy that you should apologise in person.'

Mma Ramotswe looked out of the window again. Her little white van was just being driven to the back of the garage.

'Then I must go and see her,' said Mr Molefelo.

'There is no need,' said Mma Ramotswe. 'Mma Tsolamosese has just arrived. She will be here in a moment. Are you all right, Rra?'

'I am embarrassed,' said Mr Molefelo,' But I am ready.'

♦

Mma Tsolamosese looked at the man standing in front of her.

60

'You are looking very well,' she said. 'You were thinner then. You were a boy.'

'And you were my mother. You looked after me very well.'

She smiled at him. 'I was your mother in Gaborone. You were my son while you were here. I am very proud of you now. Mma Ramotswe has told me how well you have done.'

'But I did a very bad thing to you, and I am very sorry for it.' said Mr Molefelo. 'I have never stolen anything else. That was the only time. Your radio …'

Mma Tsolamosese interrupted him. 'A radio is a small thing. A man is a big thing.'

They sat down together, and Mma Ramotswe prepared some bush tea for them. They talked about what had happened in their lives, and then Mma Ramotswe took Mr Molefelo to one side and spoke quietly to him.

'There is something you can do for this woman,' she said.

He looked over at Mma Tsolamosese. 'She is such a kind woman,' he whispered. 'I will do whatever I can.'

'There is a grandchild,' said Mma Ramotswe. 'A little girl. She may not live long because of this cruel illness. But you could do something now to make a difference to that life. You could give money to Mma Tsolamosese to use for the child. Good food, pretty clothes – these things could make her short life happy. That would certainly put right the wrong you did all those years ago.'

Mr Molefelo looked at her. 'You are right, Mma. I can do that. It is not a big thing to do.'

'Then you tell Mma Tsolamosese,' said Mma Ramotswe.

Mma Tsolamosese listened quietly to what Mr Molefelo said. Then she spoke.

'I always thought that you were a good person, Rra,' she said. 'Nothing that I have heard – nothing – has made me change my mind about you.'

She reached for his hand, and Mma Ramotswe looked away. Mr Molefelo had earned this moment for himself, and there should not be anyone watching.

Chapter 10 Two Problems Solved

Mr Molefelo had written two cheques that day: one to Mma Ramotswe, for her professional services (three thousand pula – a large sum, but he was able to afford it), and another for two thousand pula, to be sent to Mma Tsolamosese for her grandchild. There would be other cheques to write for the cost of the school for Tebogo's daughter, but as Mma Ramotswe reminded him, it was money well spent. He had corrected his past mistakes, and knowing that, he could live happily now.

Mma Ramotswe felt that she had done a good job. But her satisfaction over the Molefelo case was spoiled by the problem of Mr Bernard Selelipeng, still unsolved. It was a situation that would not go away, and she knew she had to do something about it. At least she had now decided on a plan; she had Mr Bernard Selelipeng's address and she would go and see him early that evening, soon after he arrived home from work.

She knew Limpopo Court, a new apartment building near the Tlokweng Road. She had been in one of the apartments once before, visiting a cousin, but she had not liked it much. She preferred the old, round shapes of traditional houses to these cold, modern buildings, with their hard edges and sharp roofs.

Mr Selelipeng's apartment was number 42, on the first floor. She stood outside the blue painted front door and felt unhappy and anxious. She had to say some difficult things to him, but she had agreed to act for Mma Selelipeng, and she could not break her promise. At the same time she knew that the private life of her employee, Mma Makutsi, should not be her business.

It was not her place to do anything at all about Mr Selelipeng's behaviour to her assistant. It was a difficult situation, with no easy answers.

She knocked at the door. Mr Bernard Selelipeng opened it and saw before him a large, well-built lady. He thought she looked familiar to him, but he could not remember exactly why. Who was she?

Mma Ramotswe smiled at him. She saw the expensive blue shirt and the shiny shoes.

'I have to speak to you, Rra, about an important matter. Please will you invite me in?'

Mr Selelipeng stood to one side and allowed Mma Ramotswe to enter. He pointed to a chair and invited her to sit down.

'I am not sure who you are, Mma,' he began. 'I think I have met you, but I am not sure.'

'I am Precious Ramotswe.' she said. 'I am the owner of the No.1 Ladies' Detective Agency. Have you heard of us?'

Mr Selelipeng looked surprised. 'I have heard of your agency,' he said. 'There was an interview in the newspaper the other day.'

'That was not us, Rra. That was another business. Not connected to us. The No.1 Ladies' Detective Agency is run by two women,' she continued. 'There is me – I am the manager – and there is my Assistant Detective. She came from the Botswana Secretarial College and is now working for me. I think you know her.'

Mr Selelipeng said nothing.

'She is called Mma Makutsi,' said Mma Ramotswe. 'That is the name of this lady.'

Mr Selelipeng was still silent, but Mma Ramotswe noticed how he was drumming the fingers of his right hand on the arm of the chair.

Mma Ramotswe took a deep breath. 'I know that you are seeing this lady, Rra. She has spoken of you.'

Still Mr Selelipeng said nothing.

'She was very happy when you invited her out,' she continued. 'I could tell that something good was happening in her life. And then she told me your name …'

Suddenly Mr Selelipeng interrupted. 'So,' he said. 'So why have you come to see me, Mma? I don't like to be rude, but is this any of your business? You are her boss, but you don't own her private life.'

Mma Ramotswe spoke quietly. 'I can understand how you feel, Rra. But I am doing this because I have to.'

'Why? Why do you have to come and talk to me about a private matter? You tell me that.'

'Because your wife asked me to,' said Mma Ramotswe. 'That is why.'

Mr Selelipeng was shocked. He opened his mouth to say something and then closed it again.

'You are worried, Rra? Did you not tell Mma Makutsi that you are a married man?'

Her words had the effect she expected. Mr Selelipeng looked down. He moved back in his chair and looked like a beaten man.

'I was going to tell her,' he replied quietly. 'I was going to tell her, but I have not been able to yet. I am very sorry.'

Mma Ramotswe looked into his eyes, and saw the lie. This did not surprise her; Mr Selelipeng had behaved exactly as she had expected. This man was not going to leave his wife; she could see that.

She now had the advantage. 'So, Mr Selelipeng, what do you think we should do about this? Your wife has asked me to report on your activities. I have a professional duty to her. I also have to think about the interests of my employee, Mma Makutsi. I do not want her to be hurt by you, and I can see that you have no intention of staying with her.'

'Please do not tell my wife about this,' said Mr Selelipeng. 'I am sorry about Mma Makutsi. I do not want to hurt her.'

'Why did you not think about that earlier?' asked Mma Ramotswe. She could think of other things to say to him, but she was a kind woman and the sight of this unhappy man made it difficult for her to say anything else to make him feel even worse.

'We could try to find a solution,' she said. 'We could try to make sure that Mma Makutsi is not too badly upset. I do not want her to think that you no longer love her, or that she has been seeing a married man. That would make her feel bad about herself, and I do not want that to happen. Do you understand?'

Mr Selelipeng agreed. 'I will do what you tell me to do, Mma.'

'I thought, Rra, that it might be better if you were to move back to Mochudi for a while. You could tell Mma Makutsi that you have to go away – a change of job perhaps – and that you are not giving her up because you do not love her. Then you will buy her a very fine present and some flowers. You will know what to do. But you must make sure she does not feel she is being thrown away. That would be very bad, and I would find it difficult then not to talk to your wife about this. Do you understand me?'

'I understand you very well,' said Mr Selelipeng. 'You can be sure that I will try to make it easy for her.'

Mma Ramotswe stood up, ready to leave.

'And another thing, Rra,' she said. 'I would like you to remember that in the future these things may not work out so easily for you. Please think about that.'

'There is not going to be a next time,' said Mr Bernard Selelipeng.

He watched her from his window as she walked to her little white van, and he thought, 'I have no happiness now. My wife does not love me, but she will never let me find someone else. And I am too much of a coward to walk away and live my own

'My wife does not love me, but she will never let me find someone else.'

life. And now I no longer have that lady, who was so good to me. One day I will put a stop to all this. One day.'

And Mma Ramotswe looked up the window and saw him standing there, and she thought, 'Poor man! He was wrong to lie to Mma Makutsi and now he has lost his chance of happiness with her. Why are there always these misunderstandings between men and women? Things would be so much easier if God had only made one sort of person, and the children had come by another method – with the rain perhaps.'

She was still thinking about this as she started the van. But if there were only one sort of person, would this person be more like a man, or a woman? The answer was clear, she thought. One didn't even have to think about it.

♦

They had had a lot of bad luck recently, starting with Mr JLB Matekoni's illness and the problems with the two orphan children. Then there had been Mma Makutsi's friendship with Mr Bernard Selelipeng and the arrival of Mr Buthelezi's detective agency. But it seemed to Mma Ramotswe that at last their misfortune was coming to an end.

Soon after her visit to 42 Limpopo Court, Mma Makutsi told her that Mr Bernard Selelipeng had unfortunately been called back to Mochudi. He had explained that his parents and other aging relatives needed him there to look after them. As a result he was, sadly, unable to see her very often.

'I didn't really mind,' said Mma Makutsi. 'I liked him at first, but then – well, I just lost interest in him. You know how it is.'

Mma Ramotswe was very surprised to hear this.

'I was bored with him,' Mma Makutsi explained. 'He was a very nice man in some ways, but a bit too interested in how he looked. He also just sat there and smiled at me all the time. He was definitely in love with me, which is nice, but you can get a bit bored with that sort of thing, can't you?'

'Of course,' said Mma Ramotswe, quickly.

'He used to sit there and look into my eyes,' went on Mma Makutsi. 'After some time, it made me go cross-eyed.'

Mma Ramotswe laughed. 'Some girls would like a man like that.'

'Perhaps,' said Mma Makutsi. 'But I'm looking for someone a bit more …'

'Intelligent?'

'Yes.'

'You are very wise,' said Mma Ramotswe.

'When he said that he was going off to Mochudi, I was very pleased. I said immediately that it would not be easy for us to meet, so perhaps it was best to say goodbye. He seemed surprised, but I tried to make it easy for him. So we agreed on that. He gave me a very nice present too. He said that he could get them at a special price from the company.'

Mma Makutsi took a pair of silver earrings out of a small packet and showed them to Mma Ramotswe. In the centre of each one was a very small diamond, so small that it was difficult to see it at all. He had not been very generous, thought Mma Ramotswe, but at least he did it. That was the important thing.

It was surprising, she thought, how situations could change for the better, even when everything looked so complicated.

Even more surprising, though, was the arrival later that day of Mr Buthelezi. He knocked on the door and then entered without waiting to be invited.

'You people are very busy, I hear,' he said. 'Lots of cases.'

'Yes, Rra. Now, what can we do for you today? Do you need a detective?' said Mma Ramotswe.

Mma Makutsi laughed loudly, but was silenced by a look

from Mr Buthelezi.

'Very funny, Mma,' he said. 'The truth is, I've had enough of the detective business. I don't think it's right for me.'

For a moment Mma Ramotswe was unable to speak.

'It's a very boring business, I've decided,' he continued. 'This is a small town. People in this town lead very boring lives. They have no problems to solve. It is not like Johannesburg.'

'Or New York?' asked Mma Makutsi.

'Yes,' said Mr Buthelezi. 'It's not like New York either.'

'So what are you going to do, Rra?' asked Mma Ramotswe. 'Are you going to find another business?'

'What about a driving school?' suggested Mma Makutsi. 'You would be good at that. You could call it Learn to Drive with Jesus. You would get many safe, religious people coming to you.'

'That,' said Mr Buthelezi, 'is a very good idea, Mma. You are a clever lady. Not just beautiful, but clever too.'

♦

The following week Mma Ramotswe, Mma Makutsi and Mr JLB Matekoni organised a party down by the river. They invited the two apprentices, Mma Potokwani and her husband, Mma Boko, and Mr Molefelo and his family. The apprentices made a small fire so they could cook chicken and rice. There were other groups of people there at the same time, and some of them were families with teenage daughters. After they had eaten, the two apprentices started talking to the girls.

Mr JLB Matekoni shook his head. 'What do these young people talk about?' he asked Mma Ramotswe. 'Even the religious one is talking to those girls and trying to touch them on the arm.'

'He has gone back to girls,' said Mma Makutsi. 'He will not be religious for long.'

'I thought that might happen,' said Mma Ramotswe. 'People do not change very much.'

She looked at Mr JLB Matekoni and thought that she would not like him to change at all. He was perfect as he was. There were so few good, kind men around like him, and she was lucky to have one of them. As she was thinking this, Mma Potokwani said something similar.

'How fortunate we are to have these kind friends and to be living in this place,' she said. 'We are lucky people.'

'Mma Potokwani,' said Mr JLB Matekoni, 'is that new pump of yours working well?'

'Very well,' said Mma Potokwani. 'But in one of the houses the hot water is making a strange noise. I was wondering …'

'I will come and fix it,' said Mr JLB Matekoni. 'I will come tomorrow.'

Mma Ramotswe smiled, but only to herself.

ACTIVITIES

Chapter 1

Before you read

1 Mma Ramotswe is a private detective in Botswana, and people come to her for help. What sort of problems do you think they have?

2 Look at the Word List at the back of the book. Check the meaning of new words, then answer these questions.

   a Which seven words are for people?

   b Which two words are for animals?

   c Which words would you be likely to hear often in a police station?

3 Read the Introduction. Then discuss these questions with another student.

   a How did Alexander McCall Smith get the idea for the main characters in the book?

   b Why has he written several books about Mma Ramotswe?

While you read

4 Who:

   a is the owner of Tlokweng Road
      Speedy Motors?   ....

   b is going to marry Mr JLB Matekoni?   ....

   c is Mma Ramotswe's secretary?   ....

   d kept the garage running while
      Mr JLB Matekoni was ill?   ....

5 Circle the correct word or words in *italics* in each sentence.

   a Mma Ramotswe suggests looking for a man *in a bar / at a dance / in the garage*.

   b The garage apprentices are working *just the same / less well / better* now.

   c Mma Makutsi thinks that Mma Ramotswe and Mr JLB Matekoni need to *change their bank / make more money / give up the detective agency*.

d She thinks they should open *a shop in town /
a driving school / another garage*.

e Charlie *thinks it is a good idea / thinks it is a stupid idea /
only thinks about girls*.

f *The younger apprentice / Charlie / Mma Makutsi* thinks of
a name for the driving school.

After you read

6 Work with another student and discuss some of the ways you
could help Mma Makutsi to find a better life.
Student A: You are Mr JLB Matekoni.
Student B: You are Mma Ramotswe.

7 We know that Mr JLB Matekoni is a good man. Make a list of
all the good qualities in his personality.

Chapter 2

Before you read

8 What do you think Mr JLB Matekoni will say about the driving
school idea? Do you think he will want to call it Learn to Drive
with Jesus? Can you think of a better name?

While you read

9 Complete each of the following sentences.

a Motholeli likes to .... cakes, and Puso likes
to eat them.

b Mma Ramotswe is waiting for Mr JLB Matekoni to decide
on a .... for their wedding.

c Motholeli uses a .... because she is
disabled.

d Motholeli thinks her mother did not ....
about her.

e Mma Ramotswe tells her she should be ....
of her mother.

10 Are these statements correct? Write Yes or No.

a Mr JLB Matekoni is growing potatoes in the garden.   .....

b He hears a snake behind him.   .....

c He finds a dying bird.   .....

d Puso is with some other boys. .....

e Puso has a catapult. .....

f Puso cries. .....

g The adults are not surprised by his behaviour. .....

After you read

11 Discuss these questions.

  a If you were Mma Ramotswe, what would you do next about the problems with the children?

  b Can you understand Puso's behaviour? What might the reasons for it be?

Chapter 3

Before you read

12 How do you think the children will behave the next day?

While you read

13 Underline the wrong word in each sentence and write the correct word.

  a Mma Makutsi has some good news for Mma Ramotswe. ....

  b There is a very small sign outside the new agency. ....

  c The sign on the door says: *Please knock.* ....

  d Mr Buthelezi is unhappy that there are two agencies in town. ....

14 Who:

  a watches the boy with the cows? ....

  b also likes watching cows? ....

  c watches them from the office window? ....

  d has an ostrich farm near Namibia? ....

  e came to the farm late one night? ....

After you read

15 Discuss Mr Molefelo.

  a What do you know about him?

  b What do you think the bad thing is in his past?

Chapter 4

Before you read

16 What do you think Mma Makutsi is thinking as she looks out of the window at Mma Ramotswe and Mr Molefelo?

While you read

17 Are these sentences right (✔) or wrong (✗)?

a Mma Makutsi has plenty of money. .....
b She realises that a driving school would be
   expensive. .....
c She cannot afford to buy ten typewriters. .....
d Mma Manapotsi has some typewriters that
   don't work well. .....
e Mma Makutsi doesn't want these typewriters. .....

18 Complete each sentence of Mr Molefelo's story with the correct ending, 1–5.

a 'While I was a student I met a girl ... .
b 'I was very worried about the baby ... .
c 'I knew it was a very expensive radio ... .
d 'I gave my girlfriend the money ... .
e 'She said she still loved me ... .

1) and she cried and cried.'

2) and we went together to dances at the College.'

3) but I told her I did not love her, and I pushed her away.'

4) and I decided to steal it.'

5) and could not think what to do.'

After you read

19 Work with another student. Have this conversation.

Student A: You are Mma Makutsi.

Student B: You are Mma Ramotswe.

Discuss the future of the Kalahari Typing School for Men. What problems do you think there could be? What must you organise before the classes can start? What has already been organised? Make sure you know who is going to do what!

Chapter 5

Before you read

    20 What information will Mma Ramotswe need from Mr Molefelo before she can start her search? How do you think she should begin her investigation?

While you read

    21 Choose the best word to complete the sentences.

      a Mr Tsolamosese used to work at the   .....

          1) college.

          2) prison.

          3) hospital.

      b At first, the man at the pensions office refuses to give Mma Ramotswe Mma Tsolamosese's   .....

          1) first name.

          2) phone number.

          3) address.

      c Mma Ramotswe tells him she knows all about the   .....

          1) rules.

          2) government.

          3) pension.

      d Mma Tsolamosese is living in a   .....

          1) city.

          2) village.

          3) town.

    22 Who says these words?

      a 'I will speak to the minister about it.'   ....

      b 'I told you it would work.'   ....

      c 'Some keys are not in working order.'   ....

      d 'You have very good finger control.'   ....

After you read

    23 Imagine that after the first class, Mma Makutsi telephones her friend Mma Manapotsi at the college to tell her about it. Work with another student and act out their conversation.

Chapter 6

Before you read

24 How do you think Mma Tsolamosese will feel when she hears what Mma Ramotswe has to say?

While you read

25 Put the missing word in each sentence.

  a Mma Tsolamosese fetches some .... from the house for Mma Ramotswe.

  b Two of her .... are living with her.

  c At first, she does not believe that Mr Molefelo stole the ....

  d She agrees to .... Mr Molefelo.

26 Write the correct number after each question.

  a How many nights each week do the students have their typing class?   .....

  b How many weeks will their course last?   .....

  c How many points will a perfect essay get?   .....

  d How many points will be taken off for each mistake?   .....

After you read

27 Mma Makutsi is hoping that her student will ask her to go out with him. If he does, should she go? Why (not)?

Chapter 7

Before you read

28 In this chapter Mma Ramotswe and Mr JLB Matekoni visit the orphan farm. Why do you think they are going there?

While you read

29 Write R (Mma Ramotswe), M (Mr JLB Matekoni) or P (Mma Potokwani). Who:

  a explains about the noises the pump is making?   .....

  b goes to the pump house?   .....

  c wants to know how to make the cake?   .....

  d has some advice about Puso?   .....

  e takes Puso for a ride in the van?   .....

30 Which of these sentences about Mr Bernard Selelipeng is correct? Write ✔ or ✗ next to each one.

   a He drives a car.   .....

   b He never drinks alcohol.   .....

   c He is an assistant manager in the diamond office.   .....

   d He wears a ring on his left hand.   .....

   e He lives near the garage.   .....

After you read

31 Has Mma Makutsi found her true love? What do you think of Mr Bernard Selelipeng? Discuss these questions with another student.

Chapter 8

Before you read

32 What do you already know about Mr Buthelezi? Do you think his agency will be a big problem for Mma Ramotswe? Why (not)?

While you read

33 Complete these sentences.

   a The new client says that her experience with the other detective agency was ....

   b Her husband told her that he was going for a lot of ....

   c Mr Buthelezi has told her that her husband is going to ....

   d She gives Mma Ramotswe some details and a ....

34 Where do these happen? Match the sentences with the places, 1–3.

   a Mma Makutsi and Mr Bernard Selelipeng meet.   .....

   b He puts his hand in hers.   .....

   c They meet Mma Ramotswe and Mr JLB Matekoni.   .....

      1) at the cinema

      2) outside the church

      3) in the café

35 Do you think Mma Ramotswe should tell Mma Makutsi about
Mr Bernard Selelipeng? Give your reasons.

Chapter 9
Before you read

36 What do you already know about Tebogo? What is the best
way for Mma Ramotswe to start her search?

While you read

37 Number these sentences in the correct order, 1–8.

a	Mma Boko points to Tebogo's house.	.....
b	Mma Ramotswe goes to see Tebogo.	.....
c	Mma Ramotswe asks about Tebogo.	.....
d	Mma Ramotswe wonders if Mma Makutsi knows that Mr Bernard Selelipeng is married.	.....
e	Mma Ramotswe goes to see Mma Boko.	.....
f	Mma Ramotswe gives Mma Boko a package.	.....
g	Mma Makutsi talks a lot to Mma Ramotswe about Mr Bernard Selelipeng.	.....
h	Tebogo and her daughter come out of the house.	.....

After you read

38 At the end of this chapter who do you think feels happiest,
and why?

Chapter 10
Before you read

39 Mma Ramotswe has one problem left to solve. How do you
think she can best do this?

While you read

40 Who:

a	writes cheques?	....
b	visits Limpopo Court?	....
c	has to return to Mochudi?	....
d	receives earrings?	....
e	is looking for a new business?	....
f	promises to solve a hot water problem?	....

After you read

41 Work with some other students. Imagine you are the people at the party down by the river. Decide who is which character and act out the conversations that take place.

Writing

42 At the end of the story, the Gaborone newspaper decides to interview Mma Ramotswe about the No.1 Ladies' Detective Agency. Write the report that appears in the newspaper.

43 Some people have behaved badly in this story. Who are they? Can you find reasons to excuse their behaviour?

44 Compare Mr Molefelo and Mr Bernard Selelipeng. How are their lives similar and how are they different? What differences are there in their characters?

45 Choose a character from the book and write their answer to the essay title 'The Important Things in My Life'.

46 The second group of students has now started Mma Makutsi's typing class. Write a letter from her to a friend. Explain the reasons for starting the typing school and say how successful it has been.

47 At the end of the school year, Mma Ramotswe gets reports from Motholeli and Puso's class teachers. Write their reports.

48 It is a year after the end of this story. What do you think has happened to the following characters in that time?
Mr Molefelo   Mr Buthelezi   Charlie, the apprentice

49 Explain which character from the book you would most like to meet, and why.

50 What do you think has made McCall Smith's books about Mma Ramotswe so successful around the world?

Answers for the activities in the book are available from the Penguin Readers website. A free Activity Worksheet is also available from the website. Activity Worksheets are part of the Penguin Teacher Support Programme, which also includes Progress Tests and Graded Reader Guidelines. For more information, please visit:
www.penguinreaders.com.

WORD LIST

agency (n) a business that sells a service to people or organisations

anonymous (adj) unknown to people. An *anonymous* letter is one that is not signed by the writer.

apprentice (n) someone who works for an employer for a fixed amount of time to learn a job

brochure (n) a thin book that gives information or advertises something

bush (n) in Africa, wild country that has not been cleared for farming

case (n) an event, or a number of events, that police or detectives are trying to learn more about

catapult (n) a small stick in the shape of a Y with a piece of rubber between the ends, used by children to throw stones

client (n) someone who pays for help

disabled (adj) unable to use a part of your body

divorced (adj) single after a marriage has legally ended

enquiry (n) a question asked to get information

essay (n) a piece of writing that discusses a subject

ex- (prefix) used of a past situation; your *ex*-husband, for example, used to be your husband, but isn't now

foster child (n) a child who has been taken into someone else's family for a time, but is not legally their child

guarantee (v) to promise that something will be done

investigate (v) to try to find out about something – a crime, for example

late (adj) dead

matron (n) the person in charge of nurses in a hospital or a children's home

orphan (n) a child whose parents have died

ostrich (n) a big African bird with long legs, that cannot fly

pension (n) money paid by the government or a company to someone who does not work any more because they are old or ill

per cent (n) hundredth parts of a total of one hundred; also written as %

principal (n) the person in charge of a school or college

pump (n) a machine for moving liquid into or out of something